Tales From Midhgardhur, Volume III

COLIN ANDERS BRODD

DEDICATION

UXORI CARISSIMAE MEAE

CONTENTS

ACKNOWLEDGMENTS

First and foremost, thanks go to my wonderful wife Tanya, without whom this book would never have been a possibility, and to the rest of my family for all of the love and support.

I also want to thank all of the gamers in Arizona and the great state of Rhode Island and Providence Plantations who have helped share and shape my vision of the world of Midhgardhur. The world would not be the same without all of you!

Thanks also to all of the fans and people at Channillo.com who read the "Tales from Midhgardhur" as they came out monthly! Your fandom and support made all the difference!

1. THE TRADE

"Are you sure you know what you're doing?" A chill wind blew as he spoke. We gazed down at the entrance to the caverns where the trolls were lurking out of sight.

"I know my trade," I answered grimly. I hate it when my employers question me like that. It only made things worse that these were my people, the Haleygir of Halogaland, though it had been decades since I had been to the village of Sand on the island of Sandsey. That small island had been my childhood home, and so many years later it looked even smaller to me.

At that moment, however, we stood on more dangerous ground. We had crossed the narrow strait that separated Sandsey from Bjarkarey. The name means "island of the birch trees." It sounds pretty, doesn't it? It is a pretty island. But it is also home to some very nasty trollfolk.

When I had arrived on Sandsey a few days before, I hardly recognized the village where I grew up anymore; most of the folk I knew in my youth were dead now. Funny, in a way, since I was the one who left to follow a dangerous trade. Troll hunter. They stayed to live safe, boring lives, and most of them were gone. Who says the *Nornir* do not have a sense of humor?

I am called Alfvinur Trollsbani, Alfvinur Trollslayer, and I was home again after so long abroad that I did not recognize home anymore. Nor did home recognize me.

In a way, it is a bit of a blessing for me that not many of the Haleygir around here remember me. My childhood in and around Sand was memorable, but not in a good way. Everyone used to know the story. My parents had a baby. Everything was fine at first, but then the baby grew sickly, and everyone thought the baby was going to die. But the baby did not die. The baby lived. Still sickly, still weak, the baby clung to life. For spite, it seemed.

The baby was never the same after that – cranky and mean-spirited, needlessly and thoughtlessly cruel to others, never a cheerful child. That was my infancy. And when my hair grew in, black as wrought iron, with my parents as fair-haired as any son and daughter of the Haleygir, the folk of Sand whispered that I was a changeling. That the trollfolk had come and taken their baby, and left one of their own in trade – that I had been given human form, but I was born some goblin troll-child, left to die in the human baby's place. And yet I did not die. Some of the good folk of Sand even muttered that perhaps something should be done about that . . .

My parents tried to ignore the whispers, mutters, rumors, and frowning glances. They told themselves that it could not be true, that I was their baby, that I could not be some goblin changeling left in exchange for their own child. No one wants to believe that their baby is a monster. And however horrid my infant behavior, they told themselves that it was only the monstrous behavior typical of all babies. All babies can be difficult, after all. I just happened to be especially so. So they tried to ignore the unpleasant murmurs of the other villagers. At first.

It was inevitable, perhaps, that immersed as my parents were in the rumors that swirled through the village of Sand, something of the content of such dark speculations seeped slowly into their thoughts. They could not help but think – *What if . . .?* What if it were true? What if they were raising some sort of . . . *monster?* What if their baby were actually *something else?*

They took to laying a piece of cold iron over my crib, for superstitious villagers believed that iron was inimical to trollfolk (and while cold iron *is* quite useful against some creatures, it is certainly not sovereign against *all* trollfolk, or even most of them). They touched me with cold iron often. Someone told them that salt was good against supernatural beings as well, so they sprinkled me with salt and surrounded my crib with salt, and when I was old enough to eat solid food they added salt to that. They tried a few rhymes and incantations said to be useful for dispelling curses or enchantments. None of these charms of hedge-witchery seemed to have any effect. Eventually, my parents gave up on such foolishness. I have sometimes wondered whether they would have eventually stumbled onto something that worked if they had persisted longer.

As troublesome as I was as a baby, I only became worse as I grew older. I learned to walk and talk, as children do, but I did not use either of these new skills wisely or well. I was always getting into trouble, breaking every rule my parents set for me, spitting defiant words at them. The discipline I received seemed to have little effect, and you must understand the kind of a beating a provoked Northerner might dish out, even to a child. I remained defiant.

It was worse when I began to play with other children. I was prone to violent outbursts, and often harmed my playmates. A certain amount of rough play was expected among the Haleygir, but even by their standards, my behavior was outrageous, and the parents of other children complained. Soon, I was not allowed to play with the other village children. I pretended that this did not bother me, that I preferred solitude to the company of other whiny

4

brats, but the truth was, I hated being alone. Then again, I hated almost everything. And everyone.

There were trollfolk who dwelt on Sandsey and nearby Bjarkarey, and they were a nuisance to the villagers of Sand. They would raid for livestock and food, raid for goods the primitive beasts could not make themselves. The trolls of Bjarkarey were more fierce, but they had to row across to our island in their rude little boats, little more than hollowed-out tree trunks, to raid us. Though every free person of the Haleygir is expected to bear arms and be able to defend themselves, most of the folk were not really warriors, and it was difficult to prevent these raids by the trollish monsters. When I was a small child the raids had become infrequent for a time; the villagers speculated that we had killed so many of their best fighters that they were forced to lie low and lick their wounds for a few years. But after about my tenth year, the raids began to rise in frequency and viciousness once more. I was trained with sword and spear and bow, so that I could help defend my family's *stadhir*, our farmstead, and the village when the beasts came.

If you are from a safer place, far from where such monsters dwell, you may not know much about trolls. Few humans do, to tell the truth. It is said that trolls were created by the Jotnar, the gods of the giants, as a way of countering the races of humans and *landvaettir* that had been created by the good gods, the Aesir and Vanir. Humans, *alfar, dvergar, lytlingar, huldrufolk* . . . the children of the Aesir and Vanir were given life and true souls by the gods, and given

Midhgardhur to be their world. The Jotnar wished children of their own to help seize Midhgardhur, so they took the raw elements, like rock and mud and ice, and shaped them into horrible parodies of the children of the Aesir and Vanir. Not knowing how to give them souls, the Jotnar breathed a sort of counterfeit life into their creations, a life fueled by hatred and fury and every vile impulse. The trollfolk hate the children of the Aesir and Vanir, and envy them the souls which they can never possess. There is no making peace with the trolls. They *exist* to hate humans and the *landvaettir*. They may not have souls, but they do have cruel cunning and ferocity. They can be very difficult to kill.

I became quite adept at killing the trollfolk who came to raid our *stadhir* and the village. I had a talent for it that was rare in my little village. Too many innocent people were being killed each time trolls came raiding. When a viking crew came through and offered to clear out the local nest of trolls, the villagers decided to hire them, and I volunteered to go with them.

With my help, we tracked the trollfolk back to the caves in which they dwelt. The vikings had hoped a local guide might be helpful, but I was more than just "helpful" - I was able to track the creatures with uncanny accuracy, and led the warriors straight to the stinking lair. We fell upon them by daylight, when trollfolk are at their weakest (some will even revert to the stone from which their ancestors were shaped at the touch of sunlight, but not these ones!). We slew them all with sword and spear and fire, burning the bodies as we went, and wiped out that nest. It was that nest from which the raids against Sand had been launched for the previous few months (though the vikings said it was likely that there were others on the island, let alone on nearby Bjarkarey). The little beasts had a stash of gold and silver coins of ancient mint, and though I was but a teenage boy, I received a share of the wealth.

One of the vikings – I think his name was Einarr – said I had a talent for the trade. When I asked what he meant, he raised an eyebrow and said, "Hunting trolls, of course. You have a nose for the beasts. It pays." He gestured to the handful of gold and silver I had earned. "There's more where that came from, you know!"

He was right. Trolls are subject to all the worst passions of which humans are capable, greed for wealth among them. Most of them covet shiny things, and their lairs often contain hoards of treasure for which they have no real use. A talented troll hunter can make a small fortune just by hunting and killing the creatures. I had never considered taking up any trade other than farming before, since my parents had raised me working on our *stadhir*, but this expedition against the trollfolk of Sandsey had opened up a whole new world to me. I could take up the trade and become a trollslayer.

When the vikings sailed away from Sandsey, I sailed with them. I did not stay with them long – they wished to go trade and raid along the coast of Gaunorria or some such outlandish place, and I had no wish to venture so far south, which some say is close to the realm of

Muspellsheimur, the world of the fire giants. I traveled along the coasts of Noregur, and even traveled among the Gautar and Danir. Trolls plague humans and *landvaettir* everywhere, and following the troll hunting trade can lead one almost anywhere.

There are skills I had to master, tracking and the use of weapons and such. There are tricks of the trade to be learned in any craft, and make no mistake, hunting and killing trolls is a craft of sorts. But part of the trade is native talent, something one either has inborn within them or one doesn't. I had a *sense* for the monsters. I knew how the things thought, if what they do can even be called thinking. I was a natural troll killer. I formed partnerships as needed – normally, only a fool faces trolls alone – but I was still the same awkward, antisocial fellow I had always been, and I never found close friends or family. I still hated being alone almost as much as I hated other people. But I hated trolls most of all.

I was good at my trade.

And so when I was passing through Halogaland, and I had stopped in Hrafnista for a drink, I heard rumors that a nest of trolls was making trouble a little further up the coast, and the good folk were seeking the services of a trollslayer. I traveled north, following the rumors, and was surprised when I learned the name of the settlement that sought help, for I had all but forgotten my unhappy childhood in Sand, almost forgotten the place even existed. But once I had learned that it was Sand that needed help against trollfolk, I knew I had to come home.

Sandsey and Bjarkarey are off the coast of Halogaland, about as far north as one can go and still be in Halogaland. In winter the nights are very, very long, and the *Nordhurljos,* the North-lights, unfurl across the night skies in banners of emerald fire. It is a dangerous place to live, even without the trollfolk living nearby. It was a long journey up to the isles, and each stage of the journey became increasingly more difficult as there was less and less traffic going so far up the coast. Good roads became bad roads, bad roads became rough trails. Fewer ships sailed in the direction I was going. Rather than waiting to ride with some merchant who might happen to be sailing to Sandsey, I found a fisherman who owned more than one boat and paid him in gold for a small clinker-built skiff I could sail myself.

When I had arrived in my skiff at the village of Sand, I found that although the rumors had taken a long time to travel south to Hrafnista, the villagers were still very much in need of assistance. The attacks by the trolls had grown progressively worse over the last few months, and a band of young folk who had gone off to hunt the beasts had been routed, with several of them having been killed.

I offered my services to the village council. They seemed suspicious of me at first, but there were a couple of old-timers who remembered me as a native son of Sandsey, and that I had taken part in a punitive expedition against the trolls long ago. I had left Sandsey to take up the trade of trollslayer, after all. So the old-timers vouched for me. One old man commented that my parents would have been proud of me, that I was so successful in my chosen trade. I sneered at the old fool; what could he know of how my parents would feel?

That afternoon, I visited the ruins of the farm where I had grown up and paid my respects at the graves of the man and woman who raised me. They had both died long ago; few live to great old age on Sandsey. I found that I had no tears for them, but I paid my respects just the same. I returned to the village before dark and slept in the hall maintained for the village council.

The next morning I met with remaining volunteers willing to go hunting trolls. They were mostly teenaged fools who barely knew one end of a sword or spear from the other, but as I said before, only a fool hunts trolls alone. So I took them along, although I considered the possibility that I would have been better off alone than surrounded by whelps who might accidentally stab *me* in an effort to get at the trolls. Despite the overcast sky threatening storms, I decided to get on with the business.

The young villagers who had volunteered for the troll hunting expedition had introduced themselves, but as we were preparing to depart, I realized that I had not cared enough to listen to or remember their names. Whatever. In my head, I referred to them by salient characteristics, mostly involving their hair. There was "Red" (I also thought of him as "Scar," because he had a nasty one on his cheek from an earlier, unsuccessful troll hunt), "Blondie," "Braids" (also blonde, but her hair was gathered into long, intricate braids), "Balding" (the kid could not have been more than twenty winters, and already his hairline was receding quickly), "Beard" (he was a little older, and actually had a full beard), and "Darkling" (she had dark hair like me, as rarity in those parts; I guessed that at least one of her parents had come to Noregur as a thrall from somewhere foreign). They were annoying, but I supposed that I needed them.

I took a couple of volunteers in my skiff, and one of the others borrowed a fishing boat, and we made the crossing to Bjarkarey. It was an uncommonly gloomy, misty day, and the pale white trunks of the birch trees loomed out of the fog like ghosts. Near the shore we found some of the rude dugouts used by the trollfolk, and from there I was able to find tracks and trails that led us inland. The volunteers with me seemed to jump and twitch at every sound, but at least with their absurd vigilance I could be fairly sure that the little beasts were not going to sneak up on us. Most trollfolk are reluctant to operate in daylight anyway, but on such a dark day, one could never be certain.

Whatever strange sense it was that had always helped me to hunt trolls in the past was still with me, as strong as it ever was. I was able to lead my small party without much difficulty through the mist-shrouded forest to the entrance to the caves where the trollfolk laired. There was a depression in the ground, almost a pit, ringed by birch trees that seemed twisted and deformed. There was a hole in the side of that depression large enough to a man to pass through, if he crouched a little. This was where the beasts lived. Their home.

It was then that one of the fools with me asked me if I was sure I knew what I was doing. It was Red. He was nosy. "I know my trade." I wasn't going to discuss the matter with this scar-faced whelp who barely gave me the respect I deserved. To tell the truth, I wasn't interested in discussing the matter with *anyone*.

"Let's go," I sighed, and skidded down the soft earth into the depression. I waited until I reached the bottom to draw my sword, and quickly moved out of the way in case my companions were not quite so thoughtful. I was right; the young men and women had their weapons at the ready when they began their sliding descent to join me. Predictably, some injuries occurred. Braids even managed to cut her sword hand; I'm not even sure how that was possible, since she was holding her sword in that hand. I had no patience with them. None of the wounds were very serious, fortunately, but even teenagers should be capable of reasoning that sliding out of control down a hill with sharp steel in their hands might not be a good idea.

I say "steel," but the metal of their weapons barely qualified as such. The blades they bore were heirlooms of their houses, passed down on the island from generation to generation. They had them because every Northerner is expected to bear arms in defense of themselves and their kin and tribe, but some of these kids had probably never actually used their weapons in combat. They were not maintained very well, either. Some of the swords looked rather dull, and rust spotted some of the spearheads. Fortunately, better weaponry than this is rarely needed against the trollfolk, but my own equipment was carefully, zealously maintained. A man in my trade lives or dies by his gear as much as his talent, and I intended to live.

We lit torches and entered the caves. We had Braids guarding our rear, since her wound made her mostly useless to us on the front line. We found some of the runty little goblins on guard duty near the entrance, but we quickly disposed of them. They would have been more effective if they had actually been guarding at the entrance, of course, but they were apparently the sort of troll that cannot bear to be that close to sunlight, even if they are not harmed by it. The stupid things did not have any sort of proper alarm system, so the guards we dispatched did not have any way of alerting their fellows to our arrival. So that was a piece of luck.

From there, we stormed from chamber to chamber, slaying as we went. We torched the bodies in case these were the sorts of trolls that can heal from any wound that isn't burned. They didn't look like that sort of troll to me, but you can never be too careful where such creatures are concerned. Some of the crazy little critters just charged at us like berserkers. Others tried to kill us from behind makeshift barricades, taking cover at our approach.

We killed every troll we came upon, although we took losses. Beard took a spear through his throat and choked on his own blood.

Blondie went down under a swarm of little goblin things. Braids was supposed to be guarding our rear, but somehow a troll came up behind her and hamstrung her, then slit her throat while she was down before we even knew the thing was there. Still, dozens of them died for every one of us they took. Balding and Darkling turned out to be pretty good fighters, despite their inexperience, and they learned quickly. To my surprise, Red was pretty good too, although he took some more nasty wounds and would have more scars to add to his collection. Maybe he really should have been Scar, not Red. Bah. He was still annoying, second-guessing a lot of my decisions and orders as we went, insisting we needed reinforcements.

"Shut up," I told him, "I know my trade. And your whining does not help us in any way, so keep your mouth shut." He was pretty quiet after that. Still, I caught myself hoping he would be the next to fall.

No such luck. That turned out to be Darkling, which was a shame, because I thought she was kind of pretty and had been thinking about trying to arrange a more private liaison with her at some point if we both made it out of this alive. But in a room that seemed like some sort of grotesque kitchen where the trolls prepared "meals" – and it did not seem that they were very picky about what they ate, from what we saw – a bunch of trolls with meat cleavers and roasting spits and other improvised weapons charged us. Two of them ganged up on Darkling, and while she was blocking a blow from one with her shield, the other ducked in under her defense and planted an iron spit in her ribcage. What a waste! I beheaded that troll and torched its corpse myself.

After that, Balding had had enough. He said he was going back to the boats and that he would wait for us there. If we didn't come back by nightfall, he was going to row back over to Sandsey. I expected Red would want to go with him, but the scar-faced kid seemed to think retreat would be an affront to his honor, or something. He sneered at Balding for wanting to run away. Balding didn't care. He left.

Once he was gone, I saw that Red was trembling. Some of that was anger at Balding for leaving, some might have been shakiness from blood loss (he really was going to have more scars to go with that one on his cheek, if he lived), but most of it was terror. We were deep underground in a troll nest, and now he and I were the only ones left. I have to admit, I found his weakness and fear a little amusing. I grinned at him, just to provoke him. It worked; he snarled at me in anger, then asked, "What now?"

"This way," I replied, gesturing at one of the tunnels that led deeper into the nest.

"How do you know that's the right way, you freak?" he spat.

"I told you before, I know my trade. Come on."

I knew we were close to what I sought. I could *smell* it, even over the stench of the trolls. Or maybe it wasn't smell, but some other, indefinable sense that told me. But I knew.

The chamber at the end of that tunnel was the lair of the trollfolk's shaman. Its apprentice hid behind rude furnishings while we charged the shaman, even as it chanted and called down the curses of the Jotnar upon us. Something the shaman did worked; it laid a bony claw on Red, and a flash of light stunned him and sent him reeling back, almost paralyzed, crashing to the floor. Red's skull cracked on the stone floor of the chamber, and it seemed quite possible that he was dead. I'm sure that was gratifying to the troll, but it was a mistake.

The shaman had thought Red the greater threat because Red hurled himself into battle like a berserker. The foolish troll didn't even notice that while it was busy blasting Red with sorcery, I had moved alongside it, and was in a position to slide my fine steel sword through its nasty green flesh and into its kidneys while it was preoccupied. It gasped out something that might have been a prayer to the giant-gods for protection, but if so, the Jotnar did not answer. The thing died with a rattling cough, and I wiped its nasty blood off my sword on its filthy clothing before setting its dead body alight with my torch. Just to be safe.

Keeping my eyes on where the shaman's apprentice huddled behind a crude table that had been turned on its side, I checked on Red. He was still breathing, just unconscious. Gods, what would it take to kill this kid? At least he was out. I did not really want any witnesses for this. I wanted to enjoy it.

Keeping my sword ready, I stalked over to where the shaman's apprentice lurked behind an overturned table. With my shield hand, I heaved the table out of the way. He screamed in a most satisfying way. I held my sword to his throat and rasped, "Do you know who I am?"

The shaman's apprentice was quite a bit taller than the other trollfolk in this nest, though a lifetime of living in cramped tunnels and exposure to the toxic magics of the trolls has twisted his spine and left him stooped and hunched. His eyes were startlingly blue. They had warped him into a troll, but this troll had been born human. I saw the recognition dawning in those blue eyes.

"YOU! You . . . you're the . . . the *changeling!*" he grunted. "You were supposed to die!"

"I almost did. Runt of the litter, was I? Most of us are. Oh aye, I have met a few others like me. Changelings. Trollfolk left as a trade for the human children stolen away by the goblins, left to die among the humans. Except not all of us do. *I* lived!" I jabbed with my sword for emphasis, drawing a little trickle of blood. What dripped from the wound was red and entirely human.

"Why have you come here?" demanded the shaman's apprentice.

I studied the twisted little man, shaking my head slowly. "It took me a long time to realize what I was, when I was a child," I said, "I would have known it sooner if I had heard the rumors that circulated around the time I was first left with your parents. Whatever spells your shaman used to change me so that I look human were woven well, the spell has never broken. But inside . . . inside, I *knew* I was never human. I knew I had no soul.

"It was a miserable life, outcast and exiled from my true people, living among humans who hated and feared me almost as much as they did my true kind. Because I could not dwell long in any place before the humans began to realize that there was something wrong with me. That I had no soul, no real conscience. I frightened them with my mere presence. So I had to stay on the move. I became a troll hunter, you know. I hunt my own kind for gold and glory . . . and revenge!"

"But why are you here?" asked the apprentice.

"When I heard that Sandsey had a troll problem, I hoped that hunting the nest would bring me to you. As soon as I arrived on these isles, I could sense you. Smell you, almost. The *human* my tribe traded for me. Why? Why did they do it? Why did they want you and not me? Tell me and I might spare you!"

"You . . . you were born a runt. Not expected to survive. And the shaman wanted . . . he wanted my soul. And more souls for the tribe . . ." The apprentice's eyes bulged with fear, he stammered over his words. He knew that I was about to kill him, and I could smell his fear. It smelled delicious.

"How was the shaman going to get your soul? What was he going to do with it?" I was genuinely curious.

"Nay . . . he was not going to take it from me like that, not exactly. Um . . . you see, trolls have no souls of their own . . ."

"I know that, fool!" I snapped, "Get on with it!"

"Well . . . humans have souls. Trolls do not. But . . . did you know that a *trollkyn*, the offspring of a human and a troll, is born with a soul, just like a human is? It's true. Anyone born with human blood in their veins has a soul. So . . . the shaman mated me with his daughters. Lots of *trollkyn* running around these islands with my blood in their veins and true souls in their hearts. That's why the shaman wanted me . . . why he traded you for me . . . he wanted to introduce human ancestry into the bloodlines of the tribe. Because those born with true souls have choices and powers that others do not. Options forever denied to you and your kind, because you are little more than animated stone and mud and ice granted a counterfeit spirit."

"You have powers that I do not, eh?" I grinned unpleasantly at the man who had stolen my life. "Show me. Give me some demonstration of your special powers, human!"

He groaned. "I . . . I cannot. It doesn't work like that. But . . . Look, when trolls are slain, if they don't heal from whatever slew them, then that is the end. Whatever demonic trick the Jotnar used to grant the trolls life simply fades away, like dew in the morning sunlight, and the troll is gone forever. But when someone with true life, a true soul, dies, our soul may be reincarnated, or it may seek admittance to the halls of the gods. The brave go to Asgardhur, to Valholl or Folkvangur. The drowned are claimed by Ran. The dishonored dead go to Helheimur. Other gods may open other halls to other departed souls. If the gods allow, their servants can sometimes even resurrect the dead, restoring our souls to our bodies. Some part of us is immortal, or near enough. And that immortal piece of us has more to it than any troll could ever truly understand . . ."

"Enough! I weary of your prattle!" I barked, "Do you think I truly *care* about your miserable little *soul*, whatever that is? The shaman was a fool to trade me for you. It was a poor trade. Because I am here holding a sword at your throat, and he is dead. I killed him. And now I shall kill you, too!"

"Please," he begged, "Don't do this! Let me live! I am not the one who wronged you! It was not by my choice that I was given your place and your life in this tribe! Please!"

His pathetic begging illustrated how wrong the shaman had been. A soul was a weakness, not a strength. If I had a soul, I might have been moved by pity or compassion. His pleading might have moved me, made me stray from my course and forget my purpose. But in my heart, I was a troll.

"You are so proud of your immortal soul, that it can move on to some afterlife when you die? Well, I hope you enjoy your stay in Hel's hall, for surely any man who considers himself a troll is bound to that place! Get thee to Hel's hall, fool!" With these words, I thrust my blade into the throat of the man who had stolen my life. He choked and gurgled most satisfyingly as he drowned in his own blood. As he did, I twisted the blade to inflict as much pain as I could before he finally died.

When he did die, I yanked my sword from his cooling corpse and flicked the blood off it, then wiped it on his clothes. I took my torch to set him alight. I had expected to feel more satisfaction. My long quest was over; I had my vengeance on the tribe who abandoned me and the man they had traded for me. I expected to feel . . . something. Something more. Anything, really. I had felt and unholy joy and contentment when I was killing him, as I always did when murdering someone. But it did not last. The satisfaction simply . . . *evaporated.* Left me wanting more. Hungry for more. Starving for it.

Is there no lasting joy for soulless trolls like me? Is that what we are missing, what the shaman was trying to acquire for his people? No matter. Life is not about lasting joy. Life is about taking pleasures where you can. Even if you have to kill someone to get them.

I heard a sound behind me. With a wordless snarl, I whirled

around, crouching into a defensive stance. Red. I had forgotten all about Red. He had awakened, and was climbing unsteadily to his feet. Had he heard? Did he know?

Red looked from me to the troll-like man I had just killed, and then back at me again. "Was that the last of them?" he asked in a shaky voice, "Did we get them all?"

I considered killing Red. It would be so much fun to kill him. He was wounded, weak, inexperienced; I could take him easily. He annoyed me. If I slew the insolent whelp, the pleasure would spread through my human-looking body like the warmth from a shot of strong spirits. It would be delicious, sensual, wonderful . . . But there was no lasting satisfaction in it. And if I returned to Sand without him, the villagers might grow suspicious of me and my story. But if Red came with me . . . then I had *proof.* Someone to back up my story that I had come here just to wipe out this nest of trolls, and that was exactly what I had done.

"Aye, Red, that was the last of them. Come, let us search out their hoard of treasure! We passed a room with several crude chests, I bet that the treasure is there!" I gestured for him to follow me.

"Red? That is *not* my name!" he growled. He scrubbed his hand self-consciously through his red hair; he knew why I had chosen the name.

"So? I wasn't born with the name of Alfvinur, either." I grinned.

"What? What are you talking about?" Red asked suspiciously.

"Nothing. Never mind. Come, let's find some gold, and then get back to the boat. I'm sure Balding has given up on us and taken one of the boats back to Sandsey by now, but the other should still be there. Worst case, we take the dugouts that the trollfolk use. But let's get the gold and go home, anyway." I started to walk away down the passage, whistling as if happy. But I was not happy. I was never happy, really. And though I smiled when I spoke of going home, it occurred to me that this horrid cave *was* my *real* home. And I was leaving it forever. The thought soured my frame of mind, but I refused to let it show. Not to Red.

Red picked up his fallen torch and swiftly followed me up the tunnel. "Treasure . . . treasure sounds good," he said. "Hey . . . do you need an apprentice? I would love to learn about the trade!"

Maybe I would keep Red around, after all.

2. LUCK OF THE LYTLINGAR

Come in, come in! Welcome! Sit down, please! What can I get
you? A fine choice! Here you are, then! Enjoy!

What? Aye, the rumor you heard about me is true – I *was* a
companion of the great runecaster Heruli! For years, I journeyed all
over Midhgardhur by that old wizard's side, helping him in my own

humble way, when I could. Heruli used to call me his "good luck charm," which I always found rather patronizing, to be honest, but that is what folk say of my kind, and I suppose even the great Heruli was not immune to superstition. Or perhaps there was something to it; I don't claim to know the ways of fate and fortune. I always thought that the wizard was lucky for me, not the other way around.

Me? Well, I am called Tholmann, and as you can see by my overwhelming height of three human feet tall, I am of the *lytlingar* folk. My people are *landvaettir*, land-wights, and we inhabited the lands of the North long before the coming of humans. But the *lytlingar* have long believed themselves to be the unluckiest of the *landvaettir*, for more than any other wights, we have suffered at the hands of humans. The *alfar* still dwell in the deepest forests and misty islands, the *dvergar* still carve their halls from the roots of mighty mountains, the *huldrufolk* hide in the hills and woods shunned by the race of men, but we *lytlingar* have always loved fertile fields where we can grow our crops – just like humans. Humans have always wanted our lands, and being bigger and more numerous than we "little people," humans have generally taken what they wanted from us. I'm surprised I enjoy living here in the city as much as I do, to be honest.

Don't be fooled by what it says on the sign outside! It is a matter of ironic jest among my people that you humans superstitiously believe in the "luck of the *lytlingar*." If the "little people" had any luck, we would not be the outcasts of the North, dwelling in whatever places humans have not yet bothered to drive us from in order to claim our fields. My own tale is linked to the story of my people, I can tell you that! Here, let me pull up a chair by the hearth, and I shall tell you what I mean.

My ancestors used to dwell in the south of Prytania, in the rolling hills by the rivers. That was thousands of years ago, before the humans came. When the first humans came to Prytania, Gwerryn tribes crossing the channel in search of new lands where they could hunt game and gather nuts and berries, they found us dwelling in a peaceful paradise. My people taught those Gwerryn the secrets of planting crops and raising animals, the rudiments of agriculture. Those Gwerryn became the Prytani people, for whom the island of Prytania is still called today.

The Prytani have always been respectful of us, and have never forgotten that we were the ones who taught them civilization. But the *lytlingar* have always been few, and the Prytani grew ever more numerous. They spread throughout the whole island, and while they always did their best to honor the "little people," sometimes they did encroach upon our lands. When this happened, we always sought a peaceful resolution to the conflict, which usually entailed abandoning our claims to the land. We did not want to cause trouble.

Then came the Norrani. The Norrani Imperium came from far away, across the channel to the south. Neither the Prytani nor the *lytlingar* understood the threat they represented, at first. Their merchants had begun trading with us centuries before. When their legions landed on our shores, bolstered by trollfolk auxiliaries and foul sorceries, we were caught completely by surprise. The Prytani, led by their druids, went to war. So did the *alfar* from their forests and the *dvergar* from their mountains, even the *huldrufolk* from thir hidden places. At last, even my peaceful people took up arms to oppose the Norrani. For the first time, the *lytlingar* discovered we could be fierce warriors. We were good with slings and arrows, but we did not hesitate to wade into battle with a weapon in each hand, eschewing shields. But it was all in vain. Our ferocity was for naught. The Norrani triumphed.

This was the first time my own ancestors were forcibly removed from our lands. We were the first land-wights bereft of own lands. The *alfar* retreated to their forests and their islands, the *dvergar* went back beneath their mountains, the *huldrufolk* had always had the knack of disappearing. The Prytani who resisted were slain or enslaved, and those who were willing to collaborate with the Norrani became citizens of the Imperium. They assimilated. Our rich fields were given to wealthy Norrani patricians who built their villas atop the ruins of our villages. Some *lytlingar* were captured and made slaves of the Norrani. Some were allowed to live in human towns and villages if we took up trades that were useful. But many of us, my family included, were displaced. We moved north, to less desirable, less fertile lands.

The farther north one travelled in Prytania, the more wild and savage the land became, and the weaker the grasp of the Norrani Imperium. The Norrani meant to have it all eventually, however. My family settled north of the river now called the Hymbre, in the lands protected by the Norrani city of Eboracum, as it was called then. This very city, in fact, though the name has changed more than once since that time. Further north, in Alba, raged war with the native giants and trolls. Some Gwerryn folk who had never settled down to become Prytani still dwelt up there, too – savage clans who painted themselves blue with woad and fought like furies. Eventually, the Norrani built the Giantwall to seal off the northern part of the island, what they call "Alba." The "little people" dared to hope that the Wall would bring lasting peace to the island and our people.

But the demon-haunted Norrani Imperium began to crumble within a few centuries. The Norrani may once have had some high ideals; I don't know, but I do know that they were a thoroughly corrupt empire, rotten to the core. The Gauthioth hordes besieged the Norrani heartlands, and the legions were recalled to defend the ciry of Norra itself. As far as my folk were concerned, that vile city deserved its end. The Gauthioth sacked the city and cleansed it with fire and iron; they set up their own barbaric kingdoms in the ruins of the empire. The Gaunorrani are the descendants of both peoples.

From what I understand, Heruli himself was born among the Gauthioth people before they marched south against Norra; I do not claim to understand by what powerful sorceries he is still alive so many centuries later. At the time that the Gauthioth besieged the

Imperium's heartlands, some Norrani evacuated Prytania, returning to their ancestors' homeland in the south. Others remained to try to keep their holdings in Prytania without the protection of the legions, or to carve out something for themselves in the chaos. My people had no place else to go, so we tried to carry on the best we could. Then the Ethellings arrived.

The Ethellings were barbarians, relatives of the Gauthioth who were overrunning and destroying the Norrani Imperium in the Southlands. When it became known that Prytania was no longer defended by Norrani legions, the Ethelling hordes came. The stories tell how they were held off for a time – the legendary King Urtur with his enchanted blade Calibrax, who organized a defense of Prytania by convincing the remaining Norrani people to work with the Prytanian chieftains and druids, and those *landvaettir* who could be found. For a generation, the Ethellings were driven from the island, or at least confined to the far eastern "Ethelling shore." But when King Urtur died, the Ethellings swept over the green fields of Prytania like a flood, dashing away any hope of lasting peace or safety.

Once again, the other *landvaettir* withdrew to their wild lands, and the Norrano-Prytani humans faced the same fate that the Prytani once had at the hands of the Norrani. Many were slain, some were enslaved or assimilated by the Ethellings. The survivors were mostly driven into the western extremities of the island, where small kingdoms of Prytani remain to this day. But they were a broken and displaced people, just as my own ancestors had been. And my people? Aye, once again, new conquerors came to claim our lands, and the Ethellings displaced my ancestors again. My family were forced to claim even less desirable lands up by the Giantwall. You see why the "luck of the *lytlingar*" seems a bitter joke to us? Aye, we are lucky – lucky to have survived at all, perhaps. Lucky to be able to claim a patch of barren land here or there and carve out a living, perhaps even make the land green with crops, to make our gardens bloom once more. But we are land-wights without our land, and we cannot change that fate.

And so it was that I grew up on the land in the shadow of the Giantwall. My people were governed from this city that the Ethellings called Eoforwic, which had once been the Norrani Eboracum, but we were mostly left alone as long as we paid our taxes. My people discovered that we had a talent for hiding from the "big people" when we wanted too – aye, we can blend in and disappear when we do not wish to be seen. Every so often some Ethelling lout would seek us out because they had heard that we can grant wishes, or that we all have crocks full of gold hidden away somewhere. Let me assure you that when I was growing up, my family was poor. My parents and siblings and I worked hard every day to make our poor plot of land yield enough crops to keep us alive. We do not grant wishes. We could not even grant our own wishes. We had no crock of gold; I never even saw a gold coin before I took up with Heruli.

It was a hard life, but not necessarily a miserable one. The *lytlingar* are excellent cooks, and can make delicious meals with very little food, though when more is available, we do love to feast. We love good ale (we never shared the Norrani obsession with wine, and did not miss it when they stopped importing it to Prytania), good song, good stories, good fellowship. We worked hard, but we told stories, and sang, and shared our feasts with our companions. Whatever fate the Norns may send, we "little people" have always adapted and carried on.

You humans have such short life spans, it does not surprise us that you are so bad at taking the long view of history. Every human civilization seems to assume that it will be eternal. The Prytani thought they would rule Prytania forever, but my folk remembered the time before their coming, and always assumed that there might come a time when their people were no more. The Norrani Imperium claimed to be an eternal empire, but they crumbled away, and where now is the power of Norra? Sheep and cattle graze in what was once the Forum of Norra. The Ethellings took Prytania by force, and they still call it Ethelland, but my people always expected that change would come again. So we were not particularly surprised when the Danir came.

I am not certain that I understand all of what led to the Danir invasion. I do know that the heart of it was this: that one of their kings, Ragnarr Lodhbrok, had been captured and killed by King Aella of Northymbra Rice (the very Ethelling kingdom in which I lived). The sons of this Ragnarr swore vengeance and raised the Great Army to invade Ethelland and punish the Ethellings for this treatment of their father. The longships landed on our shores to the east, and once again, invaders came to overturn the order of the human civilization on Prytania. This "Great Army" landed in Prytania in the eight hundred and sixty-fifth year from the founding of the Norrani Imperium, they ravaged the land and killed many Ethellings. This time, the *lytlingar* did not rise up to defend the island – to be honest, we were tired of the whole thing, and the Ethellings had never been any friends of ours. We tried to stay out of the way of these Danir vikings, and for the most part the Danir did not bother us much when they realized that we were not allies of the Ethellings. We escaped the worst of the looting and burning. "Luck of the *lytlingar*?" Maybe. Our situation had not really improved, but it was no worse, so I guess you could say the "little people" were lucky.

In 866 N.Y., the city of Eorforwic (which had been the Norrani Eboracum) fell to the Danir, and its name changed again, because in the mouths of the invaders, "Eoforwic" was pronounced "Jorvik." Eoforwic had been the capital of Eoforwicscir, "Eoforwic-shire," and the Danir kept it as the capital of their new Jorvikskyr. This became the heart of the Denalagu – the "Danir-law," a new kingdom where the laws of the Danir held sway, and that of the Ethellings had been swept away. The Danir claimed the best lands of the Ethellings for their own farms, and sometimes claimed a bit that had belonged to a family of *lytlingar*, though for the most part they respected our holdings. We were a bit surprised at this – humans who were not going to drive us off our own land? Unheard of! The more cynical among us claimed that we had finally been resettled in lands so poor, that no humans wanted them. And yet, many of us succeeded in making our poor plots bloom. And so the *lytlingar* were content, for the most part.

I was not content, however. The farm I had inherited from my family was failing; no arts of agriculture could avail me to break the curse of barren fields. So much for the "luck of the little people." I felt lost, hopeless, depressed – oh, I knew I would not starve, we *lytlingar* are very charitable people, and we take care of our own. But being unable to grown my own crops, enjoy my own land, I could not find happiness. I wondered what had become of the land from which my ancestors had first come, far to the south. Probably claimed by some Ethelling lord as part of his manor, if the Danir had not yet conquered them and taken it. For nearly a thousand years, the *lytlingar* of Prytania had wandered from place to place, settling where we could, anticipating the next time we would be driven out and killed in wars not of our making. We were *landvaettir*, land-wights, but we were no longer bound to our land, or any land. A people without a homeland of our own, living in exile among our conquerors. Has any people on Midhgardhur ever suffered as my people have suffered?

It was on a hot summer day in 867 N.Y. that I left my family's failing farm. My wind blew dust from my fields, where nearly nothing grew. I stepped out of my low, turf-covered home, gazed out at the ruins of my life, and walked to the road. If I turned left, the road would take me into the *lytlingar* village. I did not want to face the pitying looks of my people, however. I had my pride. As much as I wanted to drown my sorrows in ale at the tavern, I had not the coin, and I could not bring myself to face either the possibility of being denied or the possibility of being offered charity. So I took the road to the right, that led past some other outlying farms towards a small pond. I told myself that I wanted to swim in the cool waters to relieve the summer heat. But I think I really wanted to drown myself. I would not admit it, even to myself, but I had contemplated filling my pockets with heavy stones and just walking out into the pond.

In my morbid moments over the previous few days, I had imagined being at the bottom of the refreshing cool water. My bones would sit in the dark, cool water, and never be seen again. My people would wonder what had become of me, but they would never guess that I had become part of our local pond, part of the land. As it was meant to be. Such were the dark thoughts that plagued me that summer.

I went whistling along the road to the pond. I felt light, happy, even joyful, as if every weight and worry had been lifted from me. As strange as that may sound, I have since learned that it is not uncommon among those who have resolved to die. Once the decision is made, whatever depressing matters have reduced the poor soul to such a state seem inconsequential, and there is an accompanying euphoria. I have seen it among the Northern warriors, too, those berserkers who seek to die in combat so that their souls may fly to Valholl. A more cheerful band of killers you have never seen than those Northern berserkers, and their joy in life seems almost perverse to those who do not understand them. But I understand them. I have been there.

So I came whistling up to the pond, smiling and happy. It was a beautiful day, if hotter than one might like. I had planned to sit by the pond and watch the birds, swim, enjoy a nice picnic lunch that I carried in my pack, and then . . . then, I would see what I did. But I heard a voice call out to me, speaking the Theodisc language favored by most *lytlingar* living on the island of Prytania these days, though with a heavy accent I had come to associate with the Danir invaders who were now the overlords here.

"Hey, you! Little man! Hey! Will you talk to me?"

I sighed. I turned and saw the human. He was tall, even for a human, though I suppose only average for a Northerner, and he was sitting on the thick green grass by the pond, which made him look smaller. He wore rugged, sturdy garments, dusty from traveling the summer roads of Jorvikskyr, and bore a wooden staff carved with runes. He was clean-shaven, which was quite unusual among men of the North, and his hair shorn close to his scalp, which was also very odd. His eyes were a startling blue, and he was looking straight at me. Even so, I thought it possible that I could vanish from his sight if I so wished. We *lytlingar* can be very stealthy, and have ways of disappearing when you big people are about. I was about step into the underbrush and make myself disappear, but he called out again, and something in his voice made me hesitate.

"Aye, you, little one! Please, will you talk with me? I mean you no harm!"

I grunted. "I mean you no harm" - words the *lytlingar* heard from the Prytani, then the Norrani, then the Ethellings, then the Danir. We knew better. The best way to avoid trouble with humans was to avoid the humans. Still, what did it matter? This man was here, now, by my village. If I vanished, what would happen? Would Danir vikings descend upon my village and burn my people out in retribution? I did not want that on my conscience. My people might be able to disappear into the undergrowth, but our village was plainly visible, and they would lose everything if the Danir decided that *lytlingar* defiance needed to be stamped out. So as my people have always done, I hoped to buy the safety of my folk with my compliance. I walked over and sat down on the grass facing the man.

"Thank you. I am sure my people seem threatening to you. Please, I promise, I mean you no harm, little one," the man said.

"Aye," I said, "we've heard that one before, so we have, and have many songs of our sorrows to show for it. Yet I'll speak to you if you wish, big man. My name, by the way, is Tholmann, not 'little one,' if you please, big man!"

He laughed then, a deep, rich laugh. "Big man, eh? I suppose I deserve that. My apologies, Tholmann! I did not intend to offend you!"

"Well, that's better then, isn't it? And how are you called, stranger?"

The man smiled at me, his blue eyes twinkling. "You can call me Heruli."

"Can I? Meaning that 'Heruli' is not your true name, then?" I knew that I probably shouldn't pry like that, but again, it didn't seem to matter much to me just then. But he just laughed again.

"Just so," he chuckled, "Just so, indeed, for true names have power, and ought not to be lightly given. 'Heruli' will do just fine, it was a common name for my tribe, long ago."

"As you wish, Heruli," I said pleasantly, "Would you care to share my meal? I brought a bit of bread and cheese, and a little dried meat, if you're hungry. Just a small flask of water, though."

"Kind of you to offer. I brought some ale, if you would care to share." He held up a large skin that sloshed.

My mouth watered at the thought of ale. Maybe this human was not so bad, after all. "Aye, very kind, to be sure. I thank you, good

Heruli!"

So we sat and passed around the food and drink and enjoyed the calm, cool breeze off the pond. We ate in companionable silence, not speaking until our light meal was over.

When we had both enjoyed our bread and cheese and ale, I cleared my throat and said, "I have no wish to offend, but are you one of the Danir that came with the Great Army? I hear the fighting is off to the south, somewhere, and this seems an odd place to find a lone soldier . . ." I did not complete the thought. I was not really sure what I was trying to ask; I was really just hoping to prompt him into telling me something.

"Ah, well, I'm no soldier, not really," he said with a laugh, and then added, "Nor am I one of the Danir in truth. I am a runecaster, and through a confluence of my mystic arts and the vagaries of fortune, I have lived a very long life, for a human. I was born a Gauthioth long ago, before the fall of Norra. I came to Prytania with the ships of the Danir, but I am not really part of their war. Just a convenient way of reaching this island, though the war itself is not particularly convenient for anyone, I suppose. I have my own affairs that need doing, and they take me to many strange places."

"You have some wizardly business in Ethelland?" I asked incredulously. It was hard to imagine the fair green hills of Ethelland as the setting for magical doings that might occupy the runecaster's time and attention.

"Not exactly," he smiled, "Ethelland is more like a stopping point along my way. I'm going to Alba."

"Alba! That's on the other side of the Giantwall! You can't go to Alba! Um, well, I mean . . . folk simply don't cross the Wall. There are giants and trolls and savages up there. That's why the Norrani built that bloody wall and enchanted it to keep the monsters away! But I suppose if you're a wizard, you can look out for yourself . . ." I felt a little embarrassed by my initial outburst. Heruli was a runecaster. He should certainly be able to handle himself even among giants and trolls and savages, or what was the point of being a runecaster, right?

But Heruli shook his head, still smiling a little, and said, "Well, aye, I suppose I can, at that. But I was hoping to hire an assistant to accompany me on my journey."

"An assistant? Good luck, friend Heruli! I fear you'll find no one in all of Ethelland who is willing to cross the Giantwall into Alba! Everyone knows that those who go to Alba do not come back!"

Heruli said nothing for a moment, and then said, "Well, I intend to come back. I have business to attend north of the Wall, so north of the Wall I must go. I can see that finding a companion will not be so simple as I had imagined. But tell me, friend Tholmann, would *you* be willing to go with me on my journey? You have the look of one who has little left to lose, and I can pay you handsomely for your time and trouble." He held up a gold coin – the first gold coin

I ever saw in my life.

I started to protest, then fell silent. I realized that I had been planning to drown myself in a pond because I had nothing left to lose except my life. He was offering gold; I was not sure I would live to spend it, but then, what did it matter whether I died in the pond or died north of the Giantwall? Except that I had supposed that my passing in the pond would be relatively peaceful and painless, and the dangers I would face beyond the Wall in Alba would presumably involve the threat of an agonizing end. Still, if I survived, the man offered gold . . . If only he kept his word! So many times my people have accepted bargains with you humans, only to find that those of the race of man see no reason to keep their word to those they see as "half a man."

I realized that Heruli was still waiting for me to answer, still holding up that gold coin. It glittered in the afternoon sunlight. I thought of all that gold coin could buy. Certainly enough ale to drown all my sorrows for some time to come. If I lived to spend it.

"Why not?" I asked, trying to sound more cheerful than I felt. "After all, what have I got to lose?"

And so began my years of travel with Heruli. We did go north of the Wall into Alba, and faced giants and other terrors in search of some rare ingredients Heruli needed for some potion or spell. I received a goodly portion of gold from him for this – to think, I had worried whether or not the great runecaster would pay me that one gold coin, and he had intended to give me a hoard of them! He invited me to sail with him when he left Prytania, and I agreed. I never returned to my failed farm.

We journeyed together to the frozen north and through the shattered remnants of the Norrani Imperium to the south, through the exotic caliphate of Nonorra, and to even stranger realms I cannot begin to name and describe. We faced giants and dragons, savages without end, demons with no names, and all manner of horrors, yet we always came through it all alive. Heruli always treated me tolerably well, though he could be a bit patronizing, as I said. I suppose that comes with the business of being a wizard, knowing all sorts of arcane secrets of the Nine Worlds and all that. Sometimes we joined other adventurers on their quests, other times it was just the two of us. And he always called me his "good luck charm" - "luck of the *lytlingar*," as they say.

So what made me settle down back here in Jorvik? Well, I got tired of life on the road, didn't I? Heruli seemed like he was born to wander, he's been traveling for hundreds of years, and doesn't even have a home to go back to. He'll wander forever, that one. Always another spell to learn, another arcane secret to reveal, another evil to thwart. Me? I denied it for decades, but I have a longing in my bones to settle down, put down roots, enjoy some good food and drink while I still can – I think the hardest part of life on the road is the rations one eats on the trail! I'd rather face a dragon again than the horrible food one must endure on the trail to a dragon's lair!

So when we passed through Jorvikskyr again – still in the hands of the Danir these days, though who can say for how much longer? – I told Heruli I was done. I wanted to retire while I still could. And Heruli, he just had this funny little sad smile, like he had been expecting me to say that, eventually. So he paid me one last pile of gold, and I used it to buy my inn here in Jorvik. He left again, and I wish him well, wherever he may be. I'm happy to stay here in my nice, cozy inn. "The Luck of the Lytlingar" - catchy name for an inn, nay? My people may not have a homeland anymore, but I own this place, and that's enough for me. I don't miss life on the road with Heruli much. Did it cost me all I had saved? Well, I shan't be telling if I *do* have a crock of gold set aside somewhere, shall I? And whatever happens, I still have my luck!

3. PURITY

The Count's Keep in Rotomagus may have been intended as a stronghold fortress, but its current occupant, Lady Poppa of Bajocassi, was more concerned with comfort than defense. In part, this was because she did not fear attack, for she had married Hrolfur, the chief of the vikings who were considered the greatest threat to the region. But Hrolfur was far away at Kirkjuborg for the moment, and Lady Poppa ruled in Rotomagus. She plainly considered herself civilized; the Keep was luxuriously appointed with fine furnishings and works of art, a place to hold court like a Gaunorrani noble, nothing like the primitive longhouses of the viking chieftains. This was the impression the Count's Keep made on Isidore and Layla when they answered the summons of Lady Poppa.

Isidore and Layla were an unlikely pair of viking adventurers. Isidore had been born into a wealthy family of Septimania. Her father, a patron of the arts, had gone to the Urrabite town of Yazirat in the Caliphate of Nonorra seeking the new styles of poetry of the *trobadors* that some claimed had their origin in that land, and Isidore had been brought along on the expedition. At the Bayt Ul-Hikma, the great public library of Yazirat, she met Layla, the daughter of an Urrabite warlord, who was destined to be married off for politics and shut up in a *harim* with her husband's other wives. At that library, Isidore and Layla discovered that they shared a love of poetry, of romances, of stories . . . and eventually, of one another. They had run away with a Northern crew aboard the viking dragonship *Sjalfvili*, exploring the world and sailing the seas in search of adventure.

Isidore and Layla had traveled to many strange places and seen eldritch sights that beggared belief, but at this moment the business of their captain took them to the city of Rotomagus in Normannia, a thoroughly mundane place. Normannia was a coastal kingdom claimed by viking overlords, though the majority of people shared the same language and culture as Septimania, the kingdom from which Isidore's family came. To Isidore, it felt uncomfortably like being back home, and to Layla, it was like being in enemy territory, for the Normanni hated and despised *paynim*, as they called Urrabites. So Isidore and Layla had taken quarters at the Riverblood

Inn by the docks on the Sequana river, and stayed in them as much as possible, reading romances to one another and trying to keep out of trouble. They were both quite surprised when late one afternoon a courier came with a summons bearing the seal of Lady Poppa.

Isidore and Layla did not dare risk ignoring a summons from the Lady who effectively ruled the city, so they informed the captain of the *Sjalfvili* (who was occupied with his own business and did not much care if they had their own affairs to look after) and made their way to the Count's Keep as the sun was setting. They wore their finest court clothes, but they also came armed, Isidore with her Northern longsword, Layla with her graceful Urrabite scimitar. They were reluctant to walk into a potential trap of some kind unprepared. When they arrived at the gatehouse to the Keep in the deepening twilight, the guards merely glanced at the seal on their summons and admitted them, and servants showed them to a well-appointed room to wait.

The room was well-lit by lamps and candles. Isidore walked over to a large bookcase and began examining the titles. "They have a lot of really good books here, Layla. I mean, not just the religious canon of the Hierarchy, but poetry and histories and all sorts of things. You should take a look!"

"I can't. I can't relax enough to enjoy reading, right now." Layla paced around the room, then sat on a chair in front of a table upon which sat a game board. Pieces of dark hardwood and gleaming ivory were arranged on the board. She idly moved a couple of pieces in a traditional opening gambit. "Whoever lives here plays *shatranj*, or at least owns a very beautiful set. Civilized."

"Playing a game does not necessarily mean civilization," said Isidore absently as she flipped through the pages of a leatherbound volume of poetry. "The Northerners play *hefnatafl*. They say it prepared them for war." She closed the book and placed it gently back on the shelf, then chose another volume. "You just like *shatranj* because your people invented it."

"We didn't, actually," replied Layla, hand still moving pieces around the board, "It came from ancient Uryanah. My people just . . ." She looked up at servants entered the room.

"The Lady will see you now," one announced, "Follow us."

Isidore and Layla exchanged glances, and Isidore shrugged, putting back the book she had been reading. Layla stood and reset the game board, then followed. The servants led them through corridors lit by flickering torches, up a winding set of spiral stairs to a room high in one of the towers of the Keep. There were guards stationed in front of the heavy wooden door at which they stopped. A servant knocked on the portal, and a woman's voice from within called for them to enter.

The door opened to reveal a dark chamber lit only by a roaring fire in the fireplace. The windows were shuttered, and the air was stifling and humid. As Isidore and Layla entered, they noted more armed guards standing watch just inside.

As their eyes adjusted to the gloom, they realized that most of the space of the chamber was dominated by a bed piled high with thick furs. The bed was occupied by a very young boy who appeared to be asleep, yet was moaning in agony. His small face was damp with heavy sweat. On a chair beside the bed sat a blonde woman in rich silks with a silver circlet set on her brow; surely this was the lady Poppa herself. Standing in attendance were a scrawny little man in red robes and a corpulent man with a stern face in the black vestments of a presbyter of the Hierarchy.

The lady mopped at the brow of the boy on the bed with a fine linen cloth, then looked up at the women whom she had summoned. "Greetings," she said, "I am Poppa of Bajocassi, Countess of Rotomagus, wife of King Hrolfur." She gestured to the black-garbed presbyter and said, "This is Father Gordo, my chaplain. And this," with a gesture to the little red-robed man, "is my personal physician and alchemist, Malain." She turned her gaze back to the boy suffering on the bed. "And this boy is my son, Vilhjalmur, King Hrolfur's heir."

All was silent for a moment except for the boy's tortured moans, then Lady Poppa arose from her chair and turned to face Isidore and Layla. "I suppose you are wondering why I have summoned you. I would not have troubled you, except that I am desperate."

"I *still* do not understand why we are consorting with these . . . *pagans,*" interrupted Father Gordo. He glared at Isidore and Layla. "You should worry that you are inviting the wrath of Almighty Dyovis just by having them here, and at a time when He is already clearly testing you, with the illness of your son . . ."

"Enough!" said Lady Poppa sharply. "We have been over this, Father Gordo! This may be the only way!"

"I shall pray for you both," muttered the presbyter, shuffling out of the room.

Sighing deeply, Lady Poppa turned back to the young women. "Please, do not take offense at Father Gordo's words. He speaks with the voice of the Hierarchy, and few rulers can afford to ignore the voice of the church. But I fear that the good presbyter does not understand all the facts of the situation."

Isidore and Layla exchanged glances, then Layla nodded; Isidore spoke essentially the same Gaunorrani dialect as Lady Poppa, so she would speak for them. "What *is* the situation, if I may ask, my Lady?"

"My son Vilhjalmur is dying slowly, as you can see. But it is no mere illness that afflicts him, according to Malain, here. He has fallen prey to a rare and potent mystical poison, no doubt slipped into his food by assassins from the court of Karolus Simplex in Sequanaborg. My husband carved out this kingdom from lands once held by the Kingdom of Neustrasia, and if there is no heir, they may be reclaimed by Neustrasia when Hrolfur dies. My husband leads a violent life; anything could happen to him at any time. So they seek to remove my son as an obstacle, trusting that Hrolfur will get himself killed soon enough. Come here." As Isidore came forward and knelt by the sickbed of Prince Vilhjalmur, Lady Poppa took her hand and guided it to her son's forehead.

"He burns like an ember!" exclaimed Isidore. "Are you certain that this is not some disease, some plague . . .?"

"Unfortunately," replied the weary physician, "I am all too certain. If it were a mere illness, there are remedies we mighty try, certain herbs and medicines that might avail us." The red-robed man stepped forward into the light cast by the hearthfire and gazed at the dying boy. "Even the prayers of a fat hypocrite like Father Gordo might suffice in such a case," Malain continued with a sour grimace, "But I have examined the boy thoroughly, and tried everything my arts permit me to try, and I am certain that it is a foul admixture of terrible poisons!"

"But there are prayers and potions that can remove the effects of poison, surely?" said Isidore. "Why have they not been administered?"

"They *have* been administered, but it has been no use!" said the tight-lipped Lady Poppa. "Malain tells me that the mix of poisons combined with certain spells has rendered the affliction immune to our efforts to cure it."

"Then I do not know what it is you want from us, my Lady," said Isidore sadly, "for neither Layla nor I are healers. We have both learned some healing lore from our books, but I fear there is little we can do for Prince Vilhjalmur!"

"Would you care to explain, Malain?" asked Lady Poppa. "This was *your* idea, after all."

"Well," said the scrawny red-robed man, "We alchemists call the sort of poison the assassins have used here a sovereign toxin – a poison that cannot be cured by any simple means, whether healer's arts, prayers, or spells. What we need to cure it is what alchemists call a sovereign remedy – a medicine that will cure any poison, even those of mystical origin. And for that, we need a substance called *alicorn.*"

"What is *alicorn*? And what does this have to do with us?" Isidore was trying not to sound impatient, but she was becoming more and more worried as this conversation continued. If they were being asked to help cure the prince, would they be blamed if they failed and he died? What if someone were trying to frame her and Layla as the assassins?

"*Alicorn* is a mystical substance with only one source," replied the red-garbed alchemist. "The horn of what the Northerners call an *einhyrningur* – a unicorn! Unicorns represent purity, you see, and the absolute purity of a unicorn is embodied physically in the unicorn's horn, in the *alicorn*. This is why the unicorn's horn is a sovereign remedy for any and all poisons; its mystical purity defeats and negates the vile corruptions of poisons and venoms. We must have that horn!"

"I do not understand. Are you saying you want *us* to hunt down and kill an *einhyrningur*? Why? Why us?" asked Isidore.

At this, Malain's cheeks flushed a red so deep they almost matched his robes, and he looked helplessly to Lady Poppa. The lady sighed at his reaction, then took a deep breath, as though bracing herself for something thoroughly unpleasant. She turned to the two women, and they could see she was flushed with embarrassment as well. Layla and Isidore exchanged confused, worried glances.

"It seems," began Lady Poppa in a tight, uncomfortable voice, "that the lore of unicorns is very specific on some particular points. Uh, that is to say, they *are* creatures of purity. They can sense the impure. It is said that they can only be successfully approached by . . . by pure maidens. That is, uh, women who are pure. Who have never . . . never . . . never known the touch of a man. Virgins. Only virgins can catch a unicorn.

"And . . . well, even if we could find a Gaunorrani girl who was a virgin, yet old enough to hunt the unicorn, she would also have to know how to use weapons, to kill the beast and take its horn. So we cannot simply send a little girl, nor a Hierarchy nun; we need . . . warriors. And although there are plenty of viking shieldmaidens who travel through our lands these days, the Northerner women tend to be . . . well, let us just say that the *maiden* part of *shieldmaiden* is perhaps not well-deserved.

"But, well, we have heard . . . uh . . . it is said that you . . . well, you both bear swords. You travel with vikings, you fight like viking women. But . . . it is said that you are both . . . *pure,* in the way required to hunt a unicorn. That you have never known the touch of lustful men. Because . . . because . . . " The lady seemed unable to make herself say the words.

"Because we love each other, not men?" Isidore struggled to keep her voice plain.

Lady Poppa exhaled and nodded. "Your peculiar . . . *preference* . . . may yet save my son's life! Two warrior women, trained in arms, both virgins! Um, if you *are*, in fact . . . uh . . ." Lady Poppa no longer seemed a regal figure to Isidore, for her embarrassment made her as awkward as any novice monk.

Isidore glanced to at Layla, and saw inscribed upon her features a thunderstorm of rage. Her hand had strayed to the hilt of her scimitar; the move did not go unnoticed by the guards, who were firmly gripping the hilts of their own swords. Isidore tried to meet Layla's eyes and shook her head slightly, but Layla would not be silent.

"You . . . you would call us *sinners* against your god for the love we bear one another, yet you dare to ask if we are *virginal* enough to hunt magical creatures to save your son's life?" Layla could not keep the fury from her voice. "I thought among your people, such things were not to be spoken of . . ."

"We do *NOT* speak of such things!" roared Lady Poppa, who then took a step back, as though she had startled herself. "We . . . we do not. Normally. And I . . . I am *sorry* that I have offended you! I do not *like* asking this of you! I *would* not, if I had any other choice! But this is the *life* of my *son*! If he dies, my heart will break, aye, but a *kingdom* may fall! Surely you must understand . . .?"

Layla walked over to the other side of the bed and knelt down. She placed her hand on the sweat-soaked brow of the prince, and hissed in surprise at the heat of his fever. She gently wiped away the sweat with a linen cloth, then said in a low voice, "I was raised surrounded by my father's eunuch guards. I ran away before I could be placed in a man's *harim*. I have never loved a man. Only Isidore."

She stood and locked eyes with the lady, then added, "I do not know the lore of this creature you call the *einhyrningur*. It sounds like superstitious nonsense, to me. But if only one who has never known the touch of a man can hunt it, then I can hunt it. But . . . but I would not exactly call myself a *virgin*." She turned her gaze to Isidore, who saw that she was actually embarrassed to be speaking so!

The lady nodded, then glanced to Isidore, who said, "I never knew a man before I met Layla, and now I never shall. I love only her. Though . . . I, too, cannot exactly claim . . . to be . . ." Isidore felt her cheeks growing ever more red.

Lady Poppa's face twisted with distaste; she bore all the signs of someone trying not to display their deep disgust. "Enough. I understand that your . . . *preference* . . . leads you to some *unnatural* acts, but I do not want to know the details. Unless it *is* a problem . . ." She turned to Malain the alchemist, her eyebrows raised. "*Could* it be a problem? I mean, I thought I understood when you suggested that these women would be maidens and therefore *pure*, but how can they be, really? I mean . . . how could anyone be *pure* who indulges in such . . . *perversions?*"

Isidore hissed, and Layla's grip on the hilt of her scimitar tightened, shifting to a combat-ready position. The guard eased their swords in their scabbards. Isidore wanted to laugh; these men did not know her Layla, who could draw her blade and cut them down before they ever saw her move. Fortunately, Malain spoke up then and broke the tension:

"I have researched the matter as thoroughly as my meagre resources can allow, my lady, and it seems that it only matters whether or not the woman has known a man. Whether she has done anything else seems to be irrelevant, from what I can tell. There were warrior-women of ancient times east of Palnorra that had the same .

. . *inclinations* . . . as these women, and it seems they sometimes hunted unicorns. I believe these women would serve my purpose, regardless of the state of their immortal souls . . ."

"We *might* be willing to 'serve your purpose' if you stop *insulting us*," growled Isidore.

"I meant no disrespect," murmured the crimson-robed alchemist, hands spread before him in a gesture of apology.

"Enough," said Layla sharply, "This child is dying, and does not have long. He will be lost, and *soon*, if we do not help. I do not want this boy to die, be he prince or pauper, and neither does Isidore. We shall help you, though it may be that in your hatred of us you do not deserve our help, but we shall help this innocent child, who does not deserve to die, if we are able to save him. Now. You must know where the *einhyrningur* can be found, if you went to the bother of researching this, and summoning us?"

Malain nodded. "There is a dark unicorn who haunts the woods just northeast of the city. It is glimpsed but rarely, but it is surely there. It's *alicorn* can save the prince, if you can get it."

Isidore and Layla looked at one another, then back at Malain. Isidore was the one who spoke. "We can get it."

"You will help us then?" asked Lady Poppa.

"We shall." Layla's slightly accented voice was firm.

Servants escorted Layla and Isidore out of the keep, and they found their own way back to the Riverblood Inn. It was a dark, cloudy night, but they knew the way well enough. At one point a couple of ruffians emerged from the shadows, probably intending to rob them, but without speaking or breaking her stride, Layla drew her scimitar and began twirling it in lazy, deadly arcs as she walked, and the footpads melted back into the shadows and disappeared. When they arrived back at the inn, the kitchen wenches had set aside some plates of food for them, which they took back to their quarters.

Isidore threw herself down on the bed they shared, made by shoving together the two beds the inn provided, and sighed. Layla was already sorting through her gear for the the things they would need to go hunting.

"I'm better with a bow," said Layla, "I think I had better be the one to kill it. You can be the one to lure it out."

"Oh, so *I'm* the *bait*?" asked Isidore, pouting.

"You're the lure," agreed Layla, grinning. "I *always* find you alluring!"

Isidore threw a pillow at Layla, then said, "Why are we helping them? Their presbyter is almost certainly praying to Dyovis for us to fail. The queen is disgusted by the thought of us, she hates us, what we are, who we are. She's only *making use* of us. And that alchemist, Malain . . . the way he licked his lips every time he looked at us . . . I think he *enjoyed* picturing what we do, the pervert! Why are we helping people who hate us? What do we owe them?"

Layla set down the quiver of arrows she had been examining. "I said why."

"I heard what you *told* them," said Isidore, "But really? Why should be help?"

"What I said to them was true. An innocent's life is at stake." Layla went back to packing her hunting gear. "Isidore, that alchemist was wrong about one thing, at least. He said the state of our souls was irrelevant. But nothing could be *more* relevant. I don't mean the superstitions of your ancestral faith in the Hierarchy, nor the superstitions of Ul-Sirat with which I was raised, ridiculous notions that it can be a sin to love another person. Love is never a sin. *Hate* is a sin. Hating us the way Lady Poppa does, the way that presbyter does, *that* is a sin. But it is not our place, Isidore, to punish sin. It *is* our place to do the right thing. We can save a dying child – how is it even a question of whether or not we do it? Of course we do it! Because *that* is true 'purity' – purity of soul, to help those who need help, regardless of hope of reward. We do what we can, when we can, with what we have, and if they hate us, that is their loss."

Isidore was smiling at her. "I love you."

Layla smiled back. "I know. I love you too. Now help me find my good hunting arrows, these are the ones for piercing armor."

Isidore got up from the bed and started rummaging through the packs on her side of the room. "Here! The quiver was behind my bags!"

"Very well," said Layla, "Now let me tell you one more thing. The game of *shatranj* was not the only thing my people brought back from Uryanah long ago. They brought ancient lore from the lost kingdoms of the east. The women of Uryanah used to hunt one-horned beasts like this *einhyrningur* you have in this country. They come in two colors, light and dark. They are creatures of purity, as the alchemist said, but the dark ones are pure evil. He said the one in these woods is dark; so we shall be doing good by slaying this evil creature. That is good news. Because I was afraid we were going to have to kill a white unicorn, and that *would* be a terrible sin!"

Isidore was frowning. "But . . . if the creature is pure evil . . . how will that help the prince?"

"The heart of the dark unicorn may be corrupt, but its horn contains the *alicorn* needed for the sovereign remedy, just like any other unicorn. What, are evil men made of different stuff than good men?" Layla smiled. "Come on. We have monsters to slay, children and kingdoms to save!" She headed for the door.

"At night?" asked Isidore.

"It will be dawn by the time we reach the heart of the forest!" laughed Layla.

"Very well. Always an adventure with you, my love!"

4. VIKINGS & VRYKOLAKES

Olafur and Eirikur were spending another miserable night on watch just a few miles upriver from their base. They were both Vaeringar, Northerners who had sought their fortunes in the great Palnorran Empire of the south, traveling down the Vylga River to the city they called Miklagardhur. Well, the folk of the North called it that, but the city had many other names, most commonly *Argyropolis* in the Palnorran tongue - the "Silver City." Having grown tired of being treated as servants, if not slaves, by soft southern aristocrats too spoiled and weak to do their own fighting,

Olafur and Eirikur had begun traveling back up the Vylga, but had found a better opportunity for fortune and glory with the Samara river pirates. The Samara pirates raided river traffic on the Vylga from their base at the Samara bend in the river. They stationed watchmen upriver and downriver from their base, day and night, and Olafur was convinced that he and Eirikur were somehow allotted more than their fair share of watch duty.

They did not dare to have a fire or lights of any kind on night watch lest they be spotted, so it was cold and they could not enjoy hot food or a game of *hefnatafl*. They just had to sit there in the dark and keep eyes on the river churning sluggishly past their watchpoint. It had been raining in the afternoon and evening, and although this had tapered off into a misty drizzle at night, both Olafur and Eirikur were already soaked and freezing before the sun went down. They swilled heavily watered ale, for if they were caught drunk on guard duty they would face terrible punishment, and grumbled softly to one another, and were bored.

Sometime around the middle of the long, black night, Eirikur spotted something out on the water. He jabbed Olafur in the ribs with his elbow and pointed to the dark shape on the river. Olafur squinted, then whispered, "What is that? Debris from upriver?"

Eirikur shook his head and scowled. "Nay," he said after a moment, "I think - I think it is a raft of some kind. Like the barges the Vylgari use."

"But traveling at night? With no lights? What, are the Vylgari now brave enough to try to sneak past us, or mount some kind of night assault on our base? It cannot be!" Olafur turned away, but Eirikur grabbed his arm.

"Aye, but look! It *is* a barge! I can see boxes and chests on the deck!" Eirikur squinted, but could not make out much more. What little moonlight and starlight there might have been was choked off by the stormclouds above, making it nearly impossible to make out any details.

"Well, whatever it is, it is going to get caught on the Bend!" The reason the river pirates made their base on this lonely stretch of the Vylga was the Bend. The river made a sharp turn, which reduced visibility for the merchants they preyed upon, and made it difficult to navigate for slower-moving barges. Their momentum would sometimes carry them into the river banks of the Bend, instead of following the current and course of the river, leaving merchants stuck in the mud and easy targets for piracy.

"I shall check it out," said Eirikur, "I know I saw crates of some kind, so there is *something* aboard. Maybe something worth taking. You stay on watch here in case there's anyone following it down the river."

Olafur was about to object - he had been a companion of Eirikur's since their days in the Imperial Guard in Miklagardhur, but that didn't mean he trusted the man not to take more than his share if there *was* treasure aboard that barge! - but then he thought better of it. It was probably nothing, and even if it wasn't, Eirikur could hardly walk off with the whole barge. The other pirates were going to see that barge in the morning, and would question the two who had been on watch. So. Let Eirikur take the risk. Olafur shrugged and went back to his guard post as Eirikur began walking downriver to where the barge had come to rest on the Bend.

Eirikur had drawn his longsword and readied his shield as he approached the trapped barge. It was a relatively small vessel of simple design, essentially a large raft, with a small load of boxes, crates, and chests, but no cabin or structures, and no visible crew. It was eerily silent, except for the croaking of frogs and the gurgle of the swirling waters at the Bend. Wishing he had a torch, Eirikur stepped carefully onto the craft, feeling it tilt a little under his weight. Eirikur tensed, ready for an attack if there were someone hiding aboard. No attack came. He relaxed, a little - as much as the eerie scene would allow.

The viking warrior stepped forward, wincing at the creak of the boards under his boots. With the tip of his sword, he flipped the flimsy lid off a nearby crate. It seemed to be full of stinking earth, soil full of rotting fertilizer. *Why would anyone load dirt on a barge?* He knelt down to open another box, this one a stout chest. Within were some ancient gold and silver coins, a scattering of small gemstones, and some ingots that looked like iron. It was more wealth than the average peasant ever saw, but small change to a viking pirate! Still, it did make investigating the barge worthwhile, Eirikur supposed.

Eirikur then spied what looked like a human form slumped on the deck amidst the boxes. He brought his sword and shield up, but the figure was not moving. It was very still; Eirikur did not even see any sign of breathing, and the position of the limbs looked contorted, as though of someone who had died whilst writhing in agony. He moved over to it, cautiously, then jabbed at it with his swordpoint. There was no movement. Eirikur felt some of the tension melt out of his shoulders as he relaxed again. But in the darkness, he could not see any distinguishing details of the person lying dead at his feet, save that his or her clothing was a rough sort of peasant homespun in a cut that was probably Vylgari.

Eirikur did some calculations. It was nearly fifteen leagues upriver to the settlement called Vylgaria, the capital of the river Vylgari. It was very unlikely that this barge had floated fifteen leagues on the river without a crew to steer it. Maybe this dead person was a crewman who had died after guiding it most of the way here. But whose barge was it? Why were they on the river? Where were they now? Eirikur could make no sense of it. Feeling a sudden chill, he quickly retreated off the barge and went to report to Olafur at the watchpost.

When dawn came, it was golden and glorious; the clouds finally parted and the sunlight danced and dazzled on the river. When their watchpoint relief arrived, they noted the barge stuck on the banks nearby. "Any trouble?" one of them asked.

Eirikur was overcome by a fit of coughing, so Olafur spoke for him, saying, "Nay. Abandoned Vylgari barge. Eirikur checked it out last night; he saw a dead body and a lot of boxes. Some treasure. We're going to report in before we get some sleep."

"Very well. Move along." Olafur and Eirikur did.

Eirikur coughed again. "Maybe you should take it easy," said Olafur, "Out on watch all night in the freezing rain with no fire to warm our bones, we're lucky if we don't *both* catch our death!"

"I am all right," gasped Eirikur, "Let's check out that barge before we check in at the camp!"

"If you are certain that you are up to it?" said Olafur in a questioning tone.

"Do not be foolish. I shall be fine." Eirikur coughed again and spat. He scratched at an itch in his armpit. His skin felt very itchy this morning.

The two vikings approached the grounded barge. It seemed far less ominous in the golden light of dawn. The barge itself was of low quality, and the various boxes and chests that formed its cargo varied from flimy, patched-up old crates to polished chests to long boxes large enough to hold bodies. The vikings came to where the dead body lay and Eirikur reached down to turn it over so that they could see him.

Eirikur started in horror and drew back, dropping the body. His cry alarmed Olafur, who drew his blade and readied for an attack, but nothing was moving on the boat. He looked questioningly to Eirikur, whose face was twisted in horror and fear. Eirikur looked up and gasped out: *"Plague!"*

Olafur looked down at the dead Vylgari man on the deck and saw the signs of a body ravaged by plague, with huge black swellings at his neck and armpits visible through his open chest. He turned his shocked gaze to Eirikur, who was scratching at his own neck, where swellings were beginning to show.

"Olafur, what-?" Eirikur never had time to finish the question. Olafur brought his sword down on Eirikur's neck, severing his head, and then he kicked both head and corpse into the river. Holding his breath, he used his shield to shove the Vylgari corpse to the edge of the barge and off into the river as well. Plague. Eirikur had spent time close to the corpse. Then he came back and spent the night at the watchpost with Olafur. *But he clearly felt sick, and I do not feel sick*, though Olafur. *I do not have the plague. I do not have the plague. I must not.*

Olafur ran along the riverbank down to the pirate camp to inform the others.

***

The Samara pirates decided to burn the barge and all that was on it. Olafur had told them that Eirikur had reported seeing some treasure aboard, but no one wanted to risk the possibility the treasure was tainted by plague. A large force of pirates took torches and oil and marched to the spot where the barge was grounded. They doused everything in oil and set torches to it, turning the barge into a bonfire that blazed most of the day. No one reported feeling ill, and the pirates generally felt thankful that they were spared whatever terrible plague the barge had carried.

Olafur felt relieved about that. But he also felt uneasy. He was almost certain that one of the long, coffin-like crates was missing from the barge when he came back with the others to burn the barge. But who could have taken it? Could it have been his imagination? He had been so overcome with horror at the possibility of contracting the plague that he had not exactly taken time to count boxes!

Besides, Olafur was more than a little shaken by the loss of Eirikur. They had served together for a long time, Eirikur and he, in jarls' armies, in the Imperial Guard of Miklagardhur, and then as viking pirates. A long time. But the moment Olafur had realized

Eirikur was infected with the plague, he had had no choice. He had been forced to kill his friend lest the infection spread. He had no choice, but it was hard to lose a friend, much less be forced to kill one.

Olafur wearily returned to his hut. He threw himself down on the makeshift straw bed and fell asleep, dreaming of the featherbeds and sheets of Miklagardhur. He slept all day and some of the night - he did not have watch duty again for a while, thank the gods! He was awakened that night by hunger and the sound of a fist banging on the door of his hut.

Groaning, Olafur rolled out of bed and looked around groggily. It was dark; he had lit no fires or lamps, so he could not see. Olafur always made sure that he could find his way to his door in total blackness, and he started that way, then stopped. A superstition he had picked up in Miklagradhur - never answer the door the first time someone knocks! As he hesitated, the knocking sounded again against the wooden door. Sighing, Olafur made his way over to it.

Olafur cleared his throat, then barked sternly, "Who goes there?"

"It is Thorfinn Redaxe, and you had better open up, Olafur!" came the grumpy response.

Olafur lifted the bar and opened the door. Thorfinn stood there wearing his chainmail byrnie, holding his sword in one hand and a torch in the other. "Did I wake you?" he growled.

Olafur knew Thorfinn didn't really care whether or not he had been sleeping, but he nodded anyway, yawning. It was late, and very dark outside. Another cloudy, moonless night. "What is it you want, Thorfinn?"

"Did you sleep all day? Hear or see anything strange?" Thorfinn was looking at him strangely.

"I did sleep all day. So no, I neither saw nor heard anything. What is this about?" Olafur felt the hairs on the back of his neck rising in alarm. Something was wrong.

"You know Tomor the Ningul?" asked Thorfinn. Olafur nodded; everyone knew Tomor. He was a Ningul, a nomad of the eastern steppes who had been cast out of his clan and ended up joining the Samara pirates. Tomor was one of the few non-Northerners in their band.

"Well, he's dead," said Thorfinn, "Not sure how. We found his body about an hour ago just a few paces from here. This throat had been torn out; it looked like a wild animal, a bear or lion or something, had killed him. But how could an animal get into our camp without being spotted?"

"How indeed?" asked Olafur, trying to conceal his increasing feeling of panic. "Are we calling out all men to hunt for the thing?"

"Not yet," said Thorfinn sourly, "The chieftains do not want to cause a panic. They sent me to check around to see if anyone nearby heard or saw anything. They want everyone else to stay inside, for now. No sense in having us all out stabbing at each other in the dark and fog." Olafur looked out past Thorfinn into the night and saw that an unusually thick fog had indeed rolled in off the river.

"Sorry I cannot help," said Olafur, "I'm going to make some food; I haven't eaten since yesterday. I shall stay here, since that is what the chieftains wish."

Thorfinn nodded grimly. "Very well. The chieftains will ring the alarm bell if they want to call us to arms." The alarm bell was a huge bronze thing that had been looted from some eastern temple ages ago; those who had stolen it were shipping it down the Vylga to sell it, and it had been captured by the pirates. It was used as a fire alarm and call to arms for the pirate camp for decades. *Everyone* came running if that bell rang.

Olafur assured Thorfinn that he would come if the bell rang, then lit a torch from Thorfinn's before bidding him farewell and closing the door. He barred it and stood still for a moment, pondering. The sense of dread that plagued him had not lessened at all. He used the torch to light the pile of firewood he had ready in the hearth, then placed the torch in a low sconce by the door. He busied himself with arranging a kettle of water over the fire. Into it he tossed some dried meat and vegetables along with some herbs. It would make a very weak stew, but it would have to suffice. Olafur had no wish to go out into the camp at night to seek something better.

Olafur was tending to his stew when another knock sounded at the door. He stepped toward the door and waited a moment. He realized he was following the Palnorran custom of waiting for a second knock, and growled, "Damned superstitious nonsense!" He lifted the bar and flung open the door, crying, "What now?"

To Olafur's shock, the person standing in the doorway of his hut was not one of the Samara pirates. It was a woman! A beautiful woman, Vylgari by her looks and the cut of her clothes, all dressed in scarlet. Her hair was a gorgeous shade of auburn. She smiled and asked, "May I come in?" She had a Vylgari accent, but spoke flawless Thjodiskmal.

Olafur recovered from his surprise enough to draw his sword and raise it up before him. "Who are you?" he asked, "How did you get into our camp?"

"I am called Sashka," she said, "I can explain everything. May I enter?" Her nose twitched, as though she were *smelling* him. Olafur told himself she was probably just smelling the food stewing in the kettle on his hearth.

"Nay, I think not," Olafur said, waving the sword at her a little. "Something strange is going on here . . ."

"You are the one who was aboard my boat," she said suddenly. "My boatman died, and it seems we ran aground here. I need a boatman, because I cannot cross running water on my own. Perhaps you can help me." She stepped toward Olafur, who raised the sword to halt her. She glared at him, and lifted her hands as if to placate him, to convince him to lower the sword.

Then Olafur saw the claws. Her hands were not the delicate lady's hands he expected to see, by gnarled, twisted things, with long claws at the ends of her fingertips. He gasped and looked up from her hands to her face, and saw her visage blur and melt, becoming a ghastly parody of feminine beauty. There was bloody gore all around her mouth and chin, as if she had been eating a raw animal. He froze in fear.

"Ah, you *see,*" she said, "Aye, you see me as I truly am! Now you *must* serve me, or die!" Her clawed hand reached out and shoved Olafur backwards, and he fell back into his hut. She stepped in and rapidly shut and barred the door. Olafur felt the paralysis lift from his limbs and scurried backwards towards the hearth as she turned her horrid countenance towards him once more. She - *it* - was shorter than he had thought, twisted and withered, flesh cold and dead and pallid.

"*What* are you?" choked out Olafur.

"Among the Vylgari and Palnorrans, we are called *vrykolakes!*" hissed the undead thing.

A *vrykolakas.* Suddenly, with a chill as cold as the grave, Olafur remembered the origin of that superstition about answering the door on the first knock. It was said that if you answered without waiting, and the caller was a *vrykolakas,* it could claim your soul, or render you powerless. He had answered without waiting for a second knock . . .

Sashka stood over Olafur. "My kind suffer from a terrible curse," she said, "We return from the grave with a thirst for blood and death. You can see for yourself how our bodies are painfully twisted and afflicted by rot and disease. I have heard rumors that there are other kinds of vampires who are not so afflicted, but perhaps that is only a tale to give hope to the gullible. We can make ourselves appear to be our beautiful, living selves, but it is only illusion, and you saw through mine. My mere presence brings pestilence and death to those around me. That is what happened to my boatman - he spent too long too close to my corpse, and he caught the plague from me. I need a new servant, a new boatman to pilot my barge downriver to new hunting grounds. I drank dry the veins of every person in the village where I was buried, and now I thirst for new blood! Perhaps *you* can serve me . . . willingly or no!"

Sashka knelt down and spoke very close to Olafur's face; the foulness of her rotten breath made him hold his own, and he hoped that he would not catch the plague from the miasma of her stench. "You can choose to serve me," she hissed, "Or I can drink your blood and wait for you to rise from your grave, and you can serve me in death as my spawn!"

In his mind, Olafur ran through every legend he knew about the blood-drinking undead. Some said garlic repelled them, or objects of sanctity, but Olafur had no such things to hand. Sunlight was said to destroy some, but it was hours before dawn. Immersion in running water might cleanse the taint of them, but the river was too far away. That left only . . . *fire!*

Summoning all his remaining strength, Olafur lunged for the hearth and grabbed a flaming log. As Sashka shrieked at him, he took the log like a fiery brand and struck at her. What had appeared under the power of her illusion as costly scarlet clothes were in fact the ragged remnants of her burial shroud, rotted away but very, very dry. They burst into brilliant flames as Olafur's makeshift weapon touched them. Sashka thrashed about with inhuman strength, smashing holes in the walls of Olafur's hut, screeching at a volume mortal lungs could scarcely produce, but the fire was consuming her, as it was beginning to consume everything she touched. The hut was filling with foul smoke.

Olafur ripped the bar from the door and ran out of the hut, colliding with Thorfinn who had heard the commotion and come running. A keening wail erupted from the burning hut, causing both men to turn and stare into the flames. Other vikings were emerging from their own huts. Somewhere in the night that huge bronze alarm bell began to toll, alerting the pirates to the fire in their camp.

Over the days that followed, Olafur was quarantined in a hut by himself, but he did not fall ill with the plague spread by the presence of a *vrykolakas*. Among the pirates were a few Vylgari and Palnorrans who were able to relate their lore about such creatures. The pirates burned the corpse of Tomor the Ningul, for he had died from Sashka's feeding, and he might arise as a *vrykolakas* himself if his corpse were left intact. It was also said that *vrykolakes* had need of resting in their own graves, or at least their own native soil, in order to replenish their unholy strength; an extensive search of the wilds around the camp eventually turned up the well-concealed, coffin-sized crate full of foul grave soil that Olafur had noticed was missing when they burned the barge. To be certain it could not somehow renew the curse, the pirates burned that coffin, too.

Once it was clear that Olafur had been spared the plague, he was released from quarantine. The pirates hailed him as a savior - he had had the strength of will to resist the paralytic horror of the *vrykolakas'* countenance, the strength of fortitude to resist the plague it carried, the strength of perception to see past the illusion of beauty. He had fought the horror single-handed and he had won. But Olafur was never the same after that. He no longer was ordered to stand watch at night, but rather, he *voluntarily* walked the river bank each night, staring upriver, watching for another such cursed barge. The other pirated thought him mad, but Olafur did not care.

"She said she drained the veins of everyone in the village," Olafur would say, especially when he was drinking, and the sun sank low in the west bringing twilight. "If all the villagers rose again like she did, they will thirst for new blood, as she did. Eventually, some of them will have to come downriver, as she did, seeking new ports of living souls from whom they can feed, and feed, and feed . . .

5. SONS OF AEGIR, DAUGHTERS OF RAN

I have not always hated the sea. Once, the sea was my life. I was a sailor. A smuggler, to tell the truth. But that was another life, it seems. Now I live on this lonely mountaintop. I shall not leave it to go down to the fjords; not for all the plunder in Gaunorria would I do this. I shall never again go near the sea.

My family thinks it is because of that storm I survived. The storm was how it started, but the storm is not the reason that I hate the sea. Let them think it was the storm. It is easier for them, that way. Let them think me mad. Let them think they understand. For I *am* mad, and they will *never* understand, if the gods are kind.

As I have confessed, I was a smuggler before the horror that made me abandon the sea forever. It was in the years immediately after the Great Army under the command of the Ragnarssynir had invaded Ethelland. I sailed with ship called the *Hafhamarr*, the *Sea Hammer*, running new recruits and supplies from Denaland to the Denalagu. The Denalagu was the kingdom the Danir had carved out for themselves on Prytania. The Ethelling fleets tried to blockade shipments of troops or supplies from the mainland, so smuggling was dangerous business. There was no telling what the Ethellings would do if they captured us. Maybe throw us into the wyrm-pit, as they did to King Ragnarr, the atrocity that began the war in the first place.

The Ethellings are distant relatives of our people, but they have occupied the weirdling island of Prytania for several centuries now, and who can say how it has changed them? They have gone native, the lot of them. Some adopted strange Prytanian cults, or were seduced by unknown native sorceries. I always hated sailing west to Prytania. But the horror, as it happened, was closer to our own shores.

We were navigating the Jutlandshaf, that narrow sea between Denaland and Noregur, when the storm arose. It was a savage tempest, far worse than anything we could remember seeing in those waters in our lives; the seawater poured over the saxboards and threatened to send the *Hafhamarr* to the bottom. All the crewmembers were terrified; I heard fierce prayers muttered as we strove to keep the ship afloat. Was Thorr, the god of thunder and storm, angered with us for some reason? I caught sight of land through the driving rain and howling winds, and pointed it out to our captain. "Land! There is land just off our starboard bow! Let us make for land while we can!"

But the captain squinted into the gale and shook his head, crying, "Nay, lad, that is Hlesey! We'll not land there unless we have no other choice!"

"Are you mad? We *have* no other choice! We must make land or die!" Desperation filled my screams as the howling wind grew even louder.

There may be worse things than death, lad!" said the captain, but as he looked around him, he could see that the *Hafhamarr* was lost. I had spoken truly; our only hope was to make for this "Hlesey" or drown. He stared blankly for a moment, then bowed his head in acquiescence and cried, "Very well! We have no choice! Row for Hlesey! Row for your lives!"

Some men muttered prayers at this, but none wished to risk their lives to dispute the order. We all set to the oars, rowing with all our might, pitting our might and main against the raw power of the storm. The gods and *jotnar* are fierce, the elements that serve them are fierce, but what is more fierce than the hearts of our people? We wanted to *live*, and we threw all of our strength into the task!

Yet, I was puzzled as to why this island should have such a fell reputation among sailors in these waters. I had sailed to the eastern shores in my youth, and since I did not often sail west until the gold of the Ragnarssynir made it so profitable, I had never learned the tales told in that region.

Slowly - very, very slowly - our ship began to creep towards the shore of Hlesey. The winds and tides were against us, but our muscle prevailed, dragging us inch by inch towards the island. But then - disaster! A bolt of lightning struck the mast, blasting it to splinters. It took a few moments to regain our sight and hearing, for our eyes had been seared by the white flash, and the boom of the thunder shook us to our souls. When we regained command of our senses, we realized that the stroke of lightning not only destroyed the mast, but had cracked the hull. Water was pouring in; the *Hafhamarr* was doomed. Sailors began to throw themselves overboard in a panic; the wiser ones risked taking the time to cast off their chainmail byrnies and other armor, lest it drag them to the bottom.

A lot of men drowned. I did not. An older sailor named Bosi and I managed to cling to some floating wooden planks and swim to shore. We sat there shivering on the beach as the storm continued to lash us, too exhausted to seek shelter. We were alive, and no longer in danger of drowning - that was enough for us at that moment. We both fell unconscious there on the shores of Hlesey.

When Bosi and I woke up, the storm had passed. The sun was beginning to go down, and we were cold and hungry. As we were looking around for any of our fellows who might have survived the shipwreck, we heard the voices of men approaching. Bosi's face showed sheer terror, and he hissed, "We have to get out of here! *Now!* We must hide!" I started to protest - surely, the islanders would show shipwrecked sailors some hospitality? - but the look on Bosi's face silenced me. We plunged into the reeds of a marshy lagoon, heading inland towards a nearby forest.

Once we were safely concealed in that forest, Bosi stopped to watch. In the twilight, we watched men with torches and lanterns searching the shore we had recently abandoned. They were also carrying weapons. But more disturbing, to my mind, was the fact that there was something *wrong* about these men that I could not quite place. I could not seem them very clearly in the dimming light, but I thought that there was something wrong with their posture, their gait. They moved like men who have been wounded, or born deformed in some way, with a squat, bow-legged stance. Whatever was strange about them, it did not matter - they were clearly hostile. This was not a rescue party looking to save shipwrecked sailors, it was an armed patrol.

Bosi and I watched them search the shoreline, but the tides had washed away any trace of our presence, so they eventually went away satisfied. We were very quiet until we were certain that they were long gone. Whispering, we discussed a fire; although we thought we were a long way from the main village on Hlesey, the storm had soaked all the kindling and dead wood in the forest and we had no flint to get a flame going. We would have to endure the cold and wet the best we could. Bosi was clearly still terrified; he was trembling and muttering prayers to all the Aesir and Vanir.

"Tell me about Hlesey," I asked Bosi at last, "What is it about this island that has you so terrified?"

Bosi frowned and then sighed. "Ah, right, you would not know, would you? You're not from these waters." He shuddered, as if something he had just said struck him as horrific. "The folk of Hlesey are not like you and me. They are . . . different. Some folk hereabouts call them the sons of Aegir and the daughters of Ran."

"The god and goddess of the sea? Why-?" But Bosi flung up a hand to cut off my words.

"NOT gods! Remember that, if nothing else! Aegir is often spoken of as if he were a god, and his wife Ran too, but they are of the *Jotnar*, the Giants, not the Aesir, nor Vanir!" he hissed. His eyes grew wide as he realized his fury had made him speak more loudly than he intended. He took a deep breath to calm himself. Then he began again.

"They say it began long ago, before even the earliest of our people came to the North. Before the waves swallowed lost Promethea. There were colonies of the Prometheans in the North. Some were voluntary. Others were more like prisons. Places of exile. Some say that Hlesey started as such. A cult of Prometheans exiled for their beliefs to Hyperborea, as they called the North, for their worship of demonic entities they called Father Dagon and Mother Hydra. We call them Aegir, Lord of the Sea, and Ran, Lady of Drowning.

"When the earliest folk of our kind came to the North, and settlers came to Hlesey, they were hostile to the strange cultists already dwelling here. Our folk shunned them, at first. But in years of plague and famine, the cultists always had good health and plenty of fish, the blessings of their gods, so they said. And they always seemed to have plenty of money, though their coins had strange symbols on them none had ever seen before. In the end, the folk of Hlesey were seduced by the cultists. They took the cultists in, became initiates of the cult of Aegir and Ran. Forsook the true gods, the Aesir and Vanir.

"They say that the folk of Hlesey learned to call fish and other creatures from the depths of the sea by certain charms, and by dropping curiously carved stones from their ships. That strange folk came out of the water to trade with them. Finally, the cultists arranged a permanent alliance. They married off nine Northerners to the nine firstborn daughters of Ran, goddess of the drowned. The firstborn daughters of Ran could assume mortal shape like women, but also like unto fish or frogs. They had children by trollish folk of the sea. These spawn were known as *Djupir* - "Those of the Deep," the "Deep Ones." They could also mate with mortal men. From them sprang the nine clans of Hlesey. A new kind of *Djupir*, a sort of hybrid of human and inhuman."

When he stopped, I stared at him in puzzlement. "Surely that does not frighten you?" I said, "Many great heroes and champions are descended from the gods. Some say all Northerners are descended from Heimdallur, who went among us in the dawn of time under the name of Rigur. Why, Ragnarr Lodhbrok himself claimed descent from the god Odhinn. The Ragnarssynir are sons of Odhinn, by that reckoning." But I saw that he was shaking his head.

"Odhinn is one of the Aesir, king of the gods and the glorious dead, father of gods and men. Aegir and Ran are twisted monstrosities, and their spawn are monstrous freaks. The hybrid sons of Aegir and daughters of Ran are not even as human as they appear, and their appearance is quite ugly to behold, with bulging eyes, squamous skin, and misshapen limbs."

"Then we had best avoid them," I said, "Are there any other settlements on Hlesey? Any . . . normal people?" I saw Bosi's bleak look as he shook his head. *No hope for help from other islanders, then.* "How can we get away from Hlesey and back to the mainland, then? Every hand will be against us, and we have no real arms." I had a dagger at my belt, and Bosi had a handaxe at his. We were not completely helpless, but we had not the arms of true vikings at our disposal.

"I do not see how we can get away. It is said that now *all* the folk of Hlesey are cultists of Aegir and Ran, they have all taken the Oaths of Aegir. No one will help us." Bosi sounded grim, but determined. "Perhaps if we find an isolated homestead . . . They all having fishing boats, at the very least . . . But we shall have to fight them."

We took turns keeping watch that night. It was not very restful - even when it was my turn to sleep, I found my nightmares plagued by fish-like *Djupir*, men who were not true men, but who had bulging eyes and rough gills and teeth like sharks. When I was on watch, my straining ears were sure I heard movement in the darkness every few minutes, and I was armed only with my dagger. If we were attacked, I hoped I would have time to wake Bosi so that we could take a few of them with us before we were overwhelmed. But no attack came that night.

In the morning, we set off through the bleak wilderness of Hlesey, keeping the coast in sight and staying alert for the sons of Aegir and daughters of Ran. We were wet, cold, hungry, and miserable, yet we both felt that we could survive if we stayed strong. The coastline led us uphill, onto cliffs overlooking the sea, and then down again, until suddenly we emerged from a copse of trees onto a hillside overlooking a village. The place looked eerily empty, as if all the folk who lived here had vanished - *all* of them. Not a child was playing, not a fisherman at work - no one was there. But from somewhere beyond the village, we could hear a kind of primitive drumming and cries. Was the whole village attending some kind of ceremony or festival?

Bosi and I took this as a good omen. With the village deserted, we could steal a boat and be off the island before any of the villagers knew we were there. We thought our luck had changed at last, that our *hamingja* was strong. But I fear that the opposite was true, that we were accursed from the moment we set foot on that island.

We slipped down the hill as quietly as we could, in case the place was not as abandoned as it seemed, and headed to where the fishing boats were docked. As we got near the docks, however, I spotted some barrels and casks that looked like they might contain dried fish and water. We would need food and drink when we set out to see, so I signalled Bosi that I was going to check them out. He nodded and headed on towards the docks without me.

Bosi was walking to the docks, past a line of primitive huts, and he did not see a fisherman come out of one of the buildings behind him. I looked up just as it struck him in the head from behind with the butt of a spear; Bosi crumpled to the ground without a sound. I stifled the urge to scream as I watched Bosi fall, and took cover behind the barrels I had been examining. From this hiding place I watched as the man who had struck down Bosi approached him. I drew my dagger but hesitated . . .

I watched as the man - or whatever it was - used the butt of his spear to turn over Bosi's unconscious body. Something was wrong with the way the villager stood and moved, the way he walked - something batrachian about his stance and gait. I saw his face when he glanced around, looking to see if there were more of us, but I made sure he did not see me. Even so, his face was one that seemed ripped from my nightmares, with squamous patches of skin and bulging eyes. He turned back to Bosi and plucked Bosi's handaxe from his belt and tucked it into his own. Then he reached down and grabbed Bosi by his jerkin and began to drag him away in the direction of the drumming. The fellow must have been stronger than he looked, since Bosi's weight did not seem to give him any real trouble.

I crouched there behind the barrels, watching this son of Aegir dragging away my companion. I looked down at the dagger clutched in my sweaty hand. I could try to rush him, make him drop Bosi to fight me. I might even win. On a good day, I was sure I could take a simple fisherman, but he seemed inhumanly strong. And he might be able to call for help - if there were any more like him around, Bosi and I would surely die. So I waited while he dragged Bosi out of sight.

I could have fled then. Perhaps I should have. I did not owe Bosi anything; we were smugglers, pirates, outlaws - not sworn brothers or men of honor. *Wyrd* had thrown us together, not choice. Yet even as I thought about simply taking a boat and leaving, I knew I could not bring myself to do it. I needed to see if Bosi could be saved. I put some casks of food and water in a boat, and made it ready to launch as soon as I returned. Then I set off over the hill to see where the native had taken Bosi.

I saw that I was approaching another cove, like the one where the village stood, just up the coast. The drumming, cries, and an odd chanting were coming from that place. Strange standing stones crowned the hill overlooking the cove, megaliths from ancient times, carved with strange runes and symbols. Crouching low behind a menhir, I looked down over the edge of a steep cliff.

Beneath me, I saw a massive crowd of men and women whose bodies seemed twisted and out of proportion in the way that I was coming to associate with the sons of Aegir and daughters of Ran. The gathering must have comprised most of the population of the village, if not all of them, gathered on the sands of the beach and standing in the shallow waters nearby.

Behind them, the waters were tainted red with blood, and I saw the corpses of the crew from the *Hafhamarr*. They had been stripped of clothing and savagely sliced in strange and obscene ways. There was also a structure standing in the water a short distance from the shore, some kind of Cyclopean masonry that seemed as if it had risen from the floor of the sea, dripping with seaweed and slime. On it stood an altar of smooth black stone, adorned with weird carvings. Figures in robes stood before the altar, leading the chant: *"Ia, Ia, Aegir fhtagn! Ia, Ia, Ran fhtagn!"* The crowd of villagers shouted the same words in response. Aside from the names of the cruel god and goddess of the sea, I did not know these words, but they filled me with an unspeakable dread. As I looked, a screaming man, shorn of his clothing, was held down on the altar by the robed and hooded acolytes. I thought I recognized him from the *Hafhamarr*, but I could not remember his name.

They were going to kill him. And there was nothing I could do.

A robed, hooded figure turned and spoke, projecting his voice so that all would hear him. This meant that I could hear him, too. "Soon, we shall have purged all of the outsiders from our sacred island, and completed a great sacrifice to Father Aegir and Mother Ran! I have cast one of the sacred stones into the depths, and with this sacrifice, we may entice one of the servants of our gods to rise from the depths! Aye, we may summon a *skoggothur!*" It sounded like *skoggothur*, but I have never heard such a name before. I suppose in the languages of the South, it would sound more like *shoggoth.*

The crowd moaned at this name, whatever it was, but I could not say whether it was in terror or religious ecstasy. Or mayhaps some combination of the two - who can say? But as I watched, the priest conducting the rite drew a wickedly curved, serpentine blade, and slashed the throat of his prisoner. Blood poured from his jugular into the water, and with a negligent shove the priest toppled his lifeless corpse into the bay. The priest turned and raised his bloodstained dagger, shouting *"Ia! Ia!* The *skoggothur* comes! It comes!"

Behind the priest, I could see that the waters of the cove had begun to roil and bubble, as if something immense was moving under the water, rising. The horror I felt was overwhelming; at that moment I suddenly realized the danger to myself. I was in no position to help anyone; I would be lucky to escape with my own life. I had been staring stupidly down at this scene, forgetting that at any moment I might be discovered. If that happened I was sure to join the rest of my former crew as a sacrifice. I began to inch away from the edge.

Just then, I saw something that caused me to freeze in place again. The fisherman who had captured Bosi appeared, having finally dragged him to this hidden cove. At some point he had stopped to bind Bosi's hands and feet with crude rope. Bosi was awake now, screaming as he was dragged to the altar. "I captured another one of the interlopers!" croaked the fisherman. His voice did not sound entirely human.

"Let his blood and corpse feed the *skoggothur!*" cried the priest. Acolytes came forward to restrain Bosi against the altar, untying the ropes but holding him fast, stripping away his clothes. Behind them the water continued to roil, and some of the corpses were suddenly dragged under the water, as if snatched or swallowed up by something from below.

Bosi was screaming and crying. I heard him say, "By Odhinn and Thorr, release me at once! Release me, you cursed beasts!"

I looked down at the dagger still clutched in my hand. My knuckles were white on the hilt. I could try to save Bosi, but I would die. There was nothing I could do. I looked again in time to see it, the thing that has made me forswear the sea forever. Something rising from the water, gelatinous, tentacled, huge . . . I could never describe it clearly if I tried. Indeed, I am not certain that it *had* a shape. It seemed formless, inchoate. As it rose, I heard a hideous piping sound, and realized that it seemed to be issuing forth from the creature! Pseudopods or tentacles reached out in all directions at once, plucking bobbing corpses from the water and pulling them into the jellylike mass of the thing.

The priest hesitated a moment, as if uncertain whether or not the *skoggothur* would attack him and his acolytes. Then he ripped the knife down Bosi's chest, leaving him alive but bleeding heavily, and kicked Bosi back into the water. Bosi screamed, first in pain from the slash of the knife, then in terror as a gelatinous pseudopod reached out and engulfed his legs and waist. It pulled him slowly back into the mass of the creature, as he begged and pleaded with the gods to end his suffering.

At that moment, I could hold no longer back the scream that had been building inside me since I had first arrived at this cove. I howled in impotent rage and horror, a howl that scarcely seemed human to my own ears. It roared over the sound of the chanting from the cultists below and the demonic piping of the *skoggothur*. They all looked up at where I stood, high on the hilltop above them.

Then the priest pointed the bloody dagger in my direction and shouted, "Another interloper! More blood for the *skoggothur!* Bring him to the altar!"

I ran then. I am not ashamed that I ran. Had I stood to face them, I would have died. Aye, I would have won entry to Valholl, but I am not formed from the stuff from which the *einherjar*, the eternal champions of Odhinn, are made! My only regret is that there was nothing I could do to save nor avenge Bosi and the others. The *Djupir*-hybrid villagers could not scale the cliffs and hills very well at all, with the clumsiness of their misshapen limbs and strangely webbed feet and hands. I ran back down the path to the village, which thankfully still seemed to be empty. I ran until I thought my lungs would burst.

And then . . . I heard them! Over the demonic piping of the *skoggothur* (which thankfully seemed to be occupied with devouring those who had been sacrificed to it), I heard the croaking shouts and the slapping of flat, webbed feet against the sand as the villagers came running. They were going to feed me to that *thing* in the cove!

As I reached the docks, I saw a *Djupir*-hybrid blocking my path to the boats. He had a fishing spear held awkwardly in his webbed hands, and his huge eyes goggled at me balefully. His skin was rough, almost scaly, and when he grinned at me his teeth seemed almost like needles. He clearly thought he had me at his mercy - he only needed to hold me there until his fellows caught up with me. "Surrender!" he croaked.

Without thought, I raised my right hand and hurled my dagger at the hybrid with all of my strength. It tumbled through the air, and I realized my mistake - if it missed, I had no other weapon, and I would be taken prisoner and tortured before they sacrificed me to their fouls gods. Thank Thorr, my aim was true! The blade of the dagger embedded itself in the hybrid's neck. Red blood and some kind of greenish ichor poured from the wound in profusion, and the spear clattered to the boards of the docks as he clutched at his throat. I was certain that the wound was a mortal one, so I shoved past him as he stumbled and fell into the water. I could not risk being captured by my pursuers!

I quickly found the fishing boat I had earlier stocked with food and drink, and cast off. I rowed away from the village as fast as I could, despite the burning in all of my muscles and lungs, despite my utter exhaustion. I rowed with all the strength I possessed. The villagers poured onto the docks in pursuit, and some had even begun to leap into their own boats, but the piping of the *skoggothur* was growing louder and louder as its gelatinous mass heaved through the water, scooping up corpses as well as cultists that were too slow to get out of the water as it came near. With the *skoggothur* lurking in the water nearby, they did not dare to pursue me!

Of course, if the *skoggothur* had decided to chase me, there would have been nothing that could have saved me. But it seemed content to gobble up the corpses that had been dumped into the water and any villagers who were careless enough to get close. It never showed any sign of pursuing me.

Nevertheless, I didn't stop rowing until I was out of sight of Hlesey. Then I collapsed, unconscious, and did not awaken until my boat hit ground on the shores of Gautland. I woke up in the bottom of the boat, stinking of fish, sunburned, and staring up at an ancient burial mound for some Gautur hero, built along a rocky shore. I remember that I rose slowly to my feet, muscles screaming and joints aching, and began to walk inland until I reached a place where I could no longer see, hear, or smell the sea. Then I fell to my knees and thanked Thorr for deliverance from the horrors of Hlesey. I have not gone within sight of the sea since that day.

They think it was the shipwreck that made me swear off the sea and move to this mountaintop. But it wasn't just the thought of drowning, of descending down to the lightless undersea halls of Ran to serve that goddess for all eternity. Nay. It was *knowing* that those things are down there. *Djupir* that have a mockery of the shape of a man, and the formless *skoggothur*, and countless other horrors as well. They are down there. I have seen them with my own eyes. Sometimes, in my sleep, I think I hear the demonic piping of the *skoggothur* on the winds, even here. Mayhaps there is no way to run far enough away from the horror to escape it entirely. Here I stay, and I shall never return to the sea.

6. WOLFSBANE

The floorboards of the cottage creaked as Ljufvina shifted her stance. She stood alone at the table in the area used for cooking, working by firelight from the hearth, mixing ingredients carefully in an iron pot. Ljufvina was a *daudha-gydhja,* a death-priestess, what her mentor, Valka, told her a foreigner from the South had once called an "Angel of Death." Ljufvina comforted the dying, said the prayers, performed the funeral rites. All of her life, she had felt called to this holy profession. Others might think it was morbid, but Ljufvina was proud to serve the dead and dying, to provide for their last needs on Midhgardhur. But tonight was different. Tonight, she felt like a murderer.

Part of the training as a *daudha-gydhja* that Ljufvina had received from Valka had been concerning herbalism. She knew herbs that could be used for healing, herbs that could bring comfort to the dying. Herbs that were poisonous. The potion that Ljufvina was brewing tonight in that iron pot contained large doses of the plant known as *Thorshjalmur* - "Thor's helm" - known in the fallen Norrani Imperium as *aconitum*. Aconite. Wolfsbane. It was deadly, and not only to wolves, despite its Southern nickname. Ljufvina did not like to handle poisons, although it was occasionally an inescapable part of her duties, usually to ease the suffering of the dying who lingered too long on death's door. This felt different, somehow.

At last, Ljufvina finished mixing the deadly concoction and poured it carefully into a clay mug. Then she set the iron pot with the remainder of the mixture on the hearthstones. She would have to remember that the deadly mixture was there; it would not do to leave *that* lying about! She peered into the clay mug containing the mixture that she had measured out. It was a strong dose, but not necessarily lethal. Not necessarily. But it was dangerous, very dangerous. She would not be doing this if she felt she had any choice. She listened to the wind howling through the trees outside. Was there another howl on that wind? Ljufvina shuddered. She did not think so. Not yet. There was a moaning sound, but that was not the wind either. It came from a shadowed corner inside the cottage.

Despite the chill, Ljufvina opened the shutters that covered the cottage's one small window. There was no glass like some Southern windows might have; when the shutters were open, the house was directly opened to the outside air. It was cool, but did not seem cold to Ljufvina. She was not really sure, though. She had lived among the Vylgar and Rys in Permia for too long; nothing seemed cold to her after that. Here among the Vendar, who were distantly related to the Vylgar (but had more closely adopted the ways of Ljufvina's people), the weather was far milder. After Permia, *nothing* seemed cold anymore. Outside, the sun had set, plunging the forest into an inky darkness. But the moon was on the rise. A full moon. It would not be long now.

With a heavy sigh, Ljufvina closed the shutters again and walked slowly to the bed in the corner where a young girl lay tossing under heavy blankets, moaning softly. Lufvina knelt by the bed and reached out to feel the girl's forehead. It was slick with sweat and burning with fever, plastering the girl's bright red hair to her head. "Sunnifa?" she asked gently. The girl moaned more loudly. "Sunnifa? It is time. I am sorry, but it *is* time, Sunnifa!"

Sunnifa awakened with a start, eyes snapping open instantly. The girl's eyes had once been hazel, but now, in this light, they looked almost the color of amber. Like a wolf's eyes. "I can feel the Change coming!" she panted, "I - I cannot stand the pain! Oh, but it burns, Ljufvina! I must not . . . ." Her voice trailed off into a groan of agony.

"I know," said the *daudha-gydhja* sadly, "I know, and it is *time*." She reached out and offered the girl the clay mug. "Drink all of it," she said, "and you may have a chance. If it does not work, then I shall do what I can for you." She drew a dagger from a sheath at her hip. The blade had been treated with silver, a difficult and expensive process requiring some knowledge of sorcery to perform effectively, but it had been worth the high price Ljufvina had paid for it. The blade was strong, sharp steel, but had the mystical properties of silver.

"Thank you," murmured Sunnifa. "Whatever happens, I thank you!" She took the clay mug in her trembling hands, and drained the poisonous concoction that Ljufvina had prepared for her. She grimaced at the bitter flavor, but she drank the whole thing in one long pull, gulping it down. She set down the mug on the small wooden table next to her bed, then turned to look at Ljufvina, her strange amber eyes meeting the priestess' grayish blue. A moment of silence stretched while they stared at one another, then Sunnifa croaked, "I can feel it working inside me . . . but something . . . something is . . . wrong . . . ." The young girl thrashed a little, muscles twitching uncontrollably, but then she slumped back down. "I can feel it dying inside me. But it is taking me with it. I am dying. But I die free. I die free. Free!"

Ljufvina continued to kneel by Sunnifa's bed as the girl died. The various poisons Ljufvina had mixed gave the girl a chance to throw off the curse that afflicted her, but they also slowed her breathing and her heart. The potion could end the curse, but at the risk of ending her life. The *Thorshjalmur* that formed the basis of the cure was poisonous in itself, and some other toxins had been added in small doses to ease the pain of it, but they increased the risk. Ljufvina had mixed it carefully, balancing the risk and the urgent need as delicately as she could, but in the end, Sunnifa gambled and lost. Slowly, her breathing slowed to a stop. Her eyes closed and did not open again. The girl was gone.

The death-priestess waited for a while, looking for any sign that a trace of life remained within Sunnifa's body, but she was soon satisfied that the poor thing was well and truly dead. She absently murmured the words of a funeral prayer over the corpse, relief warring with guilt within her. Ljufvina had killed the girl. She had mixed the poison and handed the cup to her, watched her drink it. She felt like a murderer. On the other hand, it might have worked. It might have lifted the curse without killing Sunnifa. There had been no way to know whether the girl was strong enough to survive until they tried it. And Sunnifa had *thanked* her as she died. "I die free," she had said. She was not going to become like the thing that had killed her family. She died free of the curse.

When Ljufvina had arrived in this part of Vendland, she had heard about the tragedy in this place. A terrible beast, like a dire wolf, had come from the forest and killed a number of people. Eaten them, truth be told. One of the last attacks had been against this remote cottage. Sunnifa had been here to visit her grandparents. Sunnifa's grandmother, Afadis, had been killed and her flesh devoured by the great wolf, leaving only bloody bones. The girl's grandfather, a huntsman named Varghoss, was missing, and presumed dead and eaten as well. The beast had come for Sunnifa too, had bitten the fiery-haired young girl, but a woodsman had heard the screams and came running to the rescue. He had arrived too late for the girl's grandparents, but he had saved Sunnifa! He claimed to have severed one of the wolf's paws with his axe, but the beast had managed to escape with just three paws.

The woodsman had cared for Sunnifa until Ljufvina came to the cottage to see to Afadis' burial, and to try to locate Varghoss' corpse for burial. She had found no trace of the hunter's body. But by then, the girl was sick; the bite of the beast had become infected, and Ljufvina knew the signs. The beast had been no ordinary wolf. And without a cure, red-haired Sunnifa would become like the gray beast that had slaughtered her family. Ljufvina had helped to care for the girl, explained the situation to her, and had offered to help, if she could. They had waited, hoping that Ljufvina was wrong. But tonight the moon was rising full and yellow, and the Change had begun. Ljufvina had been correct, after all. So the potion had been

Sunnifa's last chance. Ljufvina felt like she had failed - worse, she felt like she had murdered the girl. But Sunnifa had been right. She had died free.

Not like the monster that had slain Afadis, and possibly Varghoss. That beast had been twisted by the curse that afflicted it, so that it had tried to turn Sunnifa into a creature like itself. The thing was *hamrammur*, "shape-strong" - a werewolf. That was certain. And Ljufvina was just as certain that it was coming here. Tonight. The monster would be drawn back to the cabin to try to claim Sunnifa. It would be coming soon.

Still, Ljufvina refused to be rushed. Sunnifa was dead, and she was in Ljufvina's care. Ljufvina had work to do, cleaning the body and saying the prayers, performing the rites that preserved a soul from Hel's Hall and called upon the gods to take the dead home. She was a *daudha-gydhja*. Caring for the dead was her calling. She had known it for as long as she could remember. As a child, Ljufvina had been called by a different name, but she had been Ljufvina for even longer than she had known her calling. She had seen the *daudha-gydhja* working in her village, a crone named Gunnlaug, and she had asked the old woman to train her. Gunnlaug had refused; she said that Ljufvina was not suited to become a priestess of death. Every priestess to whom she spoke agreed with Gunnlaug. No one would train Ljufvina. She was "unsuited" to become a priestess. But Ljufvina had known who and what she was, and had sought out the famous Angel of Death, Valgerdhur, called Valka by her friends.

And Ljufvina became her friend.

Valka had known about Ljufvina from the moment she laid eyes upon the aspiring priestess. Ljufvina had secrets, but Valka had seen through them the moment they met - and had kept the secrets to herself. Valka had agreed to take on Ljufvina as an apprentice, to train her in the death rites, even though she knew that Gunnlaug and the other *daudha-gydhjur* had rejected Ljufvina, and why. Valka had said that she could tell that Ljufvina had been called to serve, just as Valka herself had been. Valka's love and acceptance of Ljufvina, her mentorship and friendship, had meant more to Ljufvina than she had ever been able to express to the old woman. But the day had come when Valka had left her behind, making the long and perilous journey from the Vylga River in Permia to go home to Noregur to help a dying friend make his final crossing.

Before she left, Valka had told Ljufvina that she knew everything she needed to be a *daudha-gydhja*. All she needed was confidence in herself - the one thing, as Valka had observed, that Ljufvina had always lacked. Self-confidence.

Since that day, Ljufvina had worked to prove to herself that Valka's faith in her was justified. She had traveled the Vylga River, helping the Rys and Vylgar who were dying, burying their dead or burning them as their customs demanded. She *was* good at handling the dead; they never frightened nor horrified her as they did some folk. But she grew weary of the freezing weather of Permia, and wanted to hear her own tongue spoken rather than Vylgisk, so she had begun the journey west through Vendland towards Denaland. That journey had brought her here.

As Ljufvina pondered the path that had brought her to this forlorn cottage on this moonlit night, she heard footsteps approaching the cabin. The man made no effort to conceal his approach; he trampled twigs and leaves without concern. Ljufvina was not surprised; often those who became *hamrammur* also became overconfident, sure that their new powers protected them from harm. The *hamrammir* did not concern themselves with stealth - what did it matter if their prey knew they were coming? The footsteps Ljufvina heard were bold and unafraid.

The footsteps stopped at the door to the cottage. There was a long pause. *He's close enough to smell that she's dead*, though Ljufvina. Then, slowly, the door opened.

A tall man stood in the doorway. He was an older man, gray-haired, dressed in gray furs and animal skins. He had a rough, weathered look, with tanned skin that spoke of a life spent out of doors. He wore a quiver of arrows slung over his shoulder, and carried a bow. Several blades hung from his thick leather belt. He looked every inch a hunter. His eyes were yellow, like those of a wolf.

"So, you come at last," said Ljufvina coolly. "Varghoss, I presume?"

The hunter's face twisted into an ugly grin. "Aye," he said at last, "That *is* my name, though I do not think I know you or yours. Are you the one who killed my granddaughter?"

Ljufvina shook her head. "Nay. *You* killed her, when you bit her. I just gave her a chance to escape the curse you would have laid upon her. My wolfsbane potion freed her before she died."

The man clicked his tongue, sounding disappointed, and he frowned. The yellow eyes narrowed. "What are you called, bitch?" he said. He glared at her, sizing her up. His gaze was predatory, although Ljufvina could not say whether he hungered for her as a man hungers for a woman or as a wolf hungers for its prey. She knew that Varghoss had been deprived of his granddaughter, whom he considered to be his rightful prey. He surely intended to make Ljufvina pay dearly for that.

Swallowing her fear, she forced her voice to remain calm. "I am called Ljufvina. I am the *daudha-gydhja* who buried what was left of your wife, and I shall bury Sunnifa when we are done. I'm the one who is going to bury *you*." The huntsmen chucked nastily at that; he was not afraid of her. She had known he would not be afraid of her. "How's the paw the woodsman cut off with his axe?" she asked, hoping that he was still crippled from the wound he took as a wolf.

Varghoss lifted his left arm so that the sleeve of his coat fell back. His arm had the same tanned, leathery look as his face, but the tan ended abruptly at the wrist. Beyond the wrist, his hand was pale and smooth, like the skin of a newborn baby. He grinned. "It grew back," he laughed, "It itches a bit, and I have to cover that hand with a glove when I am in town, lest folk ask questions about it. But I guess the woodsman's axe contained no silver!"

Ljufvina hefted the dagger. "This does," she said simply.

"Bah," spat Varghoss, "You don't scare me, little girl . . . no, wait . . ." He sniffed the air. "That's not quite right, is it?" He inhales deeply, then smiled a wicked smile. "So. You are . . . different. Not quite the bitch you appear to be, are you?"

Ljufvina stiffened and glared, brandishing her silvered dagger. "You'll find out just how much of a bitch I am, Varghoss, before this night is through!"

But Varghoss was still chuckling to himself. "Ljufvina?" he asked in a taunting voice, "I think not. What is it, really? What is the boy's name? It must be . . . Ljufur, right? That's your real name, isn't it?" He laughed aloud, pleased with himself.

Ljufvina was grinding her teeth in fury. "That name is *dead.* I buried it, like I bury all the dead. As I shall bury you!" she growled, repeating her earlier threat.

Varghoss snarled, but he seemed more amused than frightened. "*You* are going to bury *me*, bitch?" he asked. He stepped towards her, and his stance subtly shifted, as if his bones were warping. He was Changing. "You are all alone out here, freak! I didn't think they even let little boys like you become *priestesses*, but maybe some old bat was sweet on you and let you dress up and play? You're a pretty boy, I'll give you that, but you're no *daudh-gydhja*!" With those words, his jaw elongated into a wolfish snout and muzzle, his teeth becoming sharp and pointed, his yellow eyes glittering.

Valka had known Ljufvina's secret. The *daudha-gydhja* had known that Gunnlaug and the other priestesses had rejected her because her parents had named her Ljufur - because her parents had believed she was their son. Only a woman could become a *daudha-gydhja*, and they had not seen her as a woman. But Valka could see who Ljufvina was. She had not even had to tell the old priestess that she had known she had wanted to become a *daudha-gydhja* almost as long as she had known she was a girl. Valka had simply accepted her. Years of Valka's acceptance and encouragement had helped Ljufvina find herself, her confidence and courage. But Varghoss' cruel words threatened to shatter all of that in an instant. She could feel the terror of this monster rising up within her, and her certainty that she could defeat Varghoss wavered at his taunts.

Varghoss the *hamrammur* stepped towards Ljufvina, spittle dripping from his wolfish jaws, fingers elongating into terrible claws. He still walked on two legs like a man, but his face and hands had become utterly bestial. He howled a long, unearthly, ululating cry that froze her blood in her veins. Ljufvina stepped backwards, towards the hearth, almost stumbling over an old wooden chair.

Varghoss surged forward, swiping at the chair, smashing it to splinters with a single, powerful blow of his awful claw. Slivers of wood rained down across the chamber, but Ljufvina kept her eyes fixed on the advancing creature.

When Varghoss opened those slavering jaws to howl again, Ljufvina moved like lightning, grabbing the iron pot from the hearth that contained the rest of the wolfsbane mixture she had made. He ignored the pain in her hands, the sizzling of her flash as she grasped the hot iron straight from the hearth. She spun and flung the potion into the open mouth of the thing that had been Varghoss. Its howl was choked off by the hot liquid splashing into its eyes and down its throat. Varghoss shook in frustration, swinging his claws wildly. To a creature like Varghoss, one of the *hamrammir*, boiling liquid splashed into his eyes and onto his face was a mere annoyance - the scalding would heal almost instantly. But the substances in the potion that went down the monster's gullet - those would begin to fight the curse itself, and poison Varghoss' body as well!

Ljufvina did not count on the potion *curing* Varghoss. To some extent, the one afflicted by the curse needed to *want* to be cured for that to work. And she did not count on the poison to kill him - the dose was too weak, and Varghoss' health was unnaturally robust as the full moon rose over the forest. He could drink venom straight from the fangs of an adder and shrug it off, she guessed. But she took advantage of his momentary blindness and confusion to slip in between those wildly swinging claws, and swipe the razor-sharp silvered blade across Varghoss' throat. The werewolf's growls of rage and surprise suddenly became a sickening, wet gurgling sound, and the massive claws flew to his neck as Varghoss tried desperately to staunch the bleeding from his jugular. The massive wolf-creature stumbled about like a drunkard, gasping wetly, trying to howl but finding its vocal cords neatly severed.

Ljufvina stood panting, trying to regain her breath from her fading terror and the exertion. Her hands hurt; she had burned them badly when she grabbed the iron pot from the hearth, but she knew recipes for salves that would soothe the burn and help the wound to heal. She coldly watched as Varghoss bled out on the cottage floor. His body had reverted back to his form as an elderly huntsman, the changes wrought by the curse having simply melted away. The firelight barely illuminated the room at this point; the hearthfire had burned down to embers, and would soon go out entirely. In the fading light, the spreading pool of blood in which Varghoss' corpse lay looked black, like spilled ink.

As the light from the embers began to yield to the darkness, Ljufvina took a deep breath then made her way to a pile of blankets in the corner across from the one where Sunnifa's corpse lay. She needed sleep. In the morning, she would perform the rites and bury both Sunnifa and her grandfather Varghoss. She would lay them to rest and pray for their souls. Sunnifa had died free, but she would have to put more effort into putting Varghoss to rest. Legend said that when the *hamrammir* were not laid to rest properly, all sorts of horrors might emerge from such an accursed body and soul. Ljufvina would not permit that to happen.

Ljufvina had no strength left to deal with the bodies tonight. Some part of her mind recoiled from the thought of spending the night in the cottage with two dead bodies, but then, the dead had never really bothered her. She was a *daudha-gydhja* - an Angel of Death.

7. UNDER THE ARENA

In the dim light of the catacombs beneath the Grand Arena, Lambi closed his eyes, since it was nearly impossible to see anyway. For a moment he sat in darkness with his eyes closed, listening to the crackle of cheap torches and letting the smoky scent of the place fill his nostrils. The savor of a flavorful yet bitter wine lingered on his tongue. It was not very good, but it had flavor, which might be the best thing that could be said for it. It might be the last drink Lambi ever had. That was the source of the name of the establishment in which he found himself.

"Don't run, Lambi!" hissed a familiar female voice. Calluna. The person he had longest known in this city. An old friend, lover, adversary. It had not been clear for some time just what Calluna and Lambi were to one another. "Lambi, if you run, they are going to send me. I shall have to hunt you down and kill you. Don't make me kill you, Lambi! Don't run!"

That clarified what Calluna and Lambi were to one another, now. They were enemies. That is what they were, now.

"Damn you, open your eyes and look at me!" Calluna whispered, "Just tell me you won't run. Say *something*!"

Lambi did open his eyes. They took a moment to adjust to the dim light of the Last Taste, the subterranean tavern in which they sat. The place was hidden in the catacombs under the Grand Arena, maintained as a haven by the Brotherhood of the Sand, sometimes known as the Sandmen, the guild to which gladiators belonged. With a sort of gallows humor typical of gladiators, they had named their secret refuge the "Last Taste." The idea was that they lived so close to death, with a grim awareness that any food or drink that passed their lips might be the last thing they tasted in this world. Oddly enough, many Sandmen claimed that meditating upon this fact tended to make the food and drink they consumed all the sweeter. Lambi did not think anything could sweeten the bitter wine in his cup.

The Last Taste took up several chambers of the catacombs, repurposed as a tavern. No one knew what the rooms had been used for originally. The furnishings were makeshift at best, and the place was never well-lit. Strategically placed cheap candles and torches kept the place in a perpetual gloom that allowed the place to function, but never be comfortable. It was never very crowded, but it was a place of occasional refuge and respite for the gladiators when they could get away from their training and other duties.

Calluna leaned in towards Lambi, recapturing his attention. She was short, even for a Southerner, with olive skin and her dark hair tied back in a severe-looking ponytail. Her dark eyes glittered in the torchlight. "Say something," she repeated more calmly. Her left hand drifted to the hilt of the dagger at her waist, though she did not seem conscious of that fact. She was leaning on her right arm, which had no hand, but ended in a stump. "Look at me, and say something."

He looked at her. He schooled his features to show no emotion; he was not certain what emotion was predominant within his breast at the moment anyway. "I make no promises, Calluna. I cannot." He thought he had the forms of the words right. They were speaking in the Palnorrani tongue, a language which Lambi found endlessly, hopelessly complex, but at least he did speak it. Calluna had never bothered to learn his native Thjodhiskmal.

"You are a Sandman, Lambi. Sandmen don't run." Calluna smiled, but it was a cold smile, false and cheerless. "Sandmen who run cease to be Sandmen. They become corpses. Fodder for the beasts." The animals that were kept under the arena for use in gladiatorial combats needed to eat, and gladiators who broke their oaths were sometimes served up to keep them fed, as well as to make sure they had a taste for human flesh. It would not do to use an animal for a fight that did not want to attack its opponent.

Lambi growled, flashing his teeth in a tight smile back at her, equally cheerless. "Don't threaten me, Calluna. I am not yours to play with, anymore." He took another sip of bitter wine from his cup, and instantly regretted it. It was terrible wine. Almost sour. He grimaced, then gestured to her left hand hovering by her dagger. "Are you going to use that? Cut my throat?"

Calluna scowled at him, then relaxed. "Not if I can help it. Let me help you, Lambi. Don't run. You took an oath. I know your people don't break oaths. Don't do it. Let me help." At the end, her voice had softened, taking on a more pleading tone. He knew she really did not want to kill him. He also knew she would do it without hesitation if she believed there was no other way.

Lambi felt a surge of anger, despite Calluna's attempts to placate him and his realization that she still had feelings for him. She *dared* to speak of oaths? He forced himself to speak very slowly and deliberately, lest his fury make him stumble in the labyrinthine syntax of the accursed Palnorrani language. "They made promises to me, as you well know. They promised me my freedom. They have broken their oaths. Should I keep my word to those who have no intention of ever keeping their own?" With that, he stood to depart.

Calluna looked up at him, still seated, eyes like pools of shadow in the dim light of the Last Taste. "I understand that you are angry," she said quietly, "and that you feel that you have been treated unfairly. But the world is an unfair place. It profits you nothing to get angry at the world for being unfair. Think about what I said. I can help. But only if you hold to your oaths."

Lambi did not respond, but walked out of the Last Taste without so much as a glance back at Calluna. Everyone moved to get out of the path of the pale-skinned giant as he stalked away from the woman. *She is going to be a problem,* he thought.

***

Lambi remembered the day he had arrived in the city very clearly, despite the passage of several years. He had been brought in chains, a prisoner of legionary soldiers who had captured him in the territories they called the Vylgari Marches. Though he was not Vylgari himself, he had been a mercenary in the employ of some Vylgar rebels who opposed the Palnorran Empire. He had been knocked unconscious in an ambush, taken prisoner, and dragged hundreds of miles to the city where he still resided, the capital of the Palnorran Empire. When he arrived, that had been the day it had all started. That had also been the day that he met Calluna.

He had not been prepared for the splendor of the city of his captors. He had visited large settlements in the North, and even some cities in his travels southward before his capture. The legion that had taken him prisoner had dragged him through some drab and dreary Palnorran cities that inspired only contempt in Lambi. No city was like this one. No city could be.

The looming fortifications, while larger than Lambi had seen elsewhere, were a normal feature of city life in the South. But once through the gates, he was awed by everything - the brightly colored marbles and gaily colored paints, the soaring columns of the temples and the huge domes and beautiful balustrades on terraces overlooking the seas. Beyond the sheer physical grandeur of the place, he was struck by the vast crowd of humanity in all its kinds, with every color of skin and hair and eye, dressed in the garments of a hundred different lands, filling the marketplace with a chorus of strange languages. The smells of exotic foods cooking with spices from far-flung empires taunted the Northerner's growling stomach with the promise of meals, even if they were of foods previously unknown to him. It was like nothing Lambi could have imagined. Well did his people call the city Mikligardhur, which simply meant "Great Settlement" in Thjodhiskmal - a study in the power of understatement!

Lambi still remembered vividly his awe and bewilderment as the soldiers who kept him chained marched him through this astonishing metropolis for the first time. To this day, Lambi still did not know the true name of the city, if it even possessed such a thing. Most commonly, the Palnorrani called the city Argyropolis, which meant "Silver City" in their tongue. The Norrani Imperium, the Golden Empire, had split centuries before into Western and Eastern Empires, and the Western Empire, the Golden Empire, had fallen. The decaying and decadent remnant of the Imperium that remained in the East was nicknamed the Silver Empire after the fall of the West, and that nickname had stuck. Centuries later, it was all but officially the Silver Empire, with its capital known as the Silver City. It was said that everything in that debauched place had its price, and even a person's soul could be reckoned and valued at a certain rate in silver somewhere in the city. To the subjects of the Empire, it was truly the City of Silver.

They took him to a wide plaza in the shadow of the vast amphitheater that he would soon learn was the Grand Arena. The Noranni had introduced the idea of blood sports when their Imperium was at its height, and the Palnorrans had learned well from their former masters. Such bloodthirsty entertainments kept the populace amused and docile. His captors quickly sold the lot of prisoners (which included Lambi) to the *mangones*, the slave-dealers, who quickly re-sold him as part of a larger combined lot to representatives of the Purple Faction, which he was to learn was one of several sporting factions that participated in sporting events for the entertainment of the people of Mikligardhur. Lambi understood none of what was said during this process, for he spoke nothing of the Palnorrani tongue at that time, although he could more-or-less follow what was transpiring - he observed large amounts of money changing hands and solemn nods and handshakes as the transactions were completed. The representatives of the faction that had purchased Lambi and the rest of his lot dispatched some *lanistae*, trainers, to evaluate the new slaves. One was a Vaeringi, one of the Northerners who served the Palnorran state, which was how Lambi came to begin learning the local language. One of the *lanistae* was Calluna.

Calluna had not changed much in the intervening years, but Lambi could remember how much younger she looked as she paced in front of the prisoners - the *slaves* - and assigned them their duties. Many in the lot were malnourished Vylgar, and did not merit much attention - the beautiful one-handed *lanista* coldly consigned them to be victims of wild beasts in cheap shows for the lowest classes. But when she came to Lambi, she stopped and gazed admiringly at the pale Northerner's mighty thews. Through the Vaeringi interpreter, she asked his name. Lambi growled an answer, prompting a brief exchange between the woman and the interpreter, followed by light laughter.

"Why does she laugh?" grunted Lambi.

The Vaeringi, still chuckling, told him, "I told her that your name was Lambi, and how this is similar to our word for the lamb in our language. Calluna told me that she hoped you would be more of a lion than a lamb in the arena! Very funny!"

"Calluna? That is her name? Hmph. She assigns warriors to fight for the amusement of the rabble who live in this place?"

The Vaeringi scowled at this. "If you are wise, you will not speak ill of Calluna," he said, "but aye, she is your *lanista* - your trainer. She will teach you how to be a gladiator - what you call a warrior who fights for entertainment, though you must realize that you will be a slave, not a free warrior in the sense that you are used to. At least at first!"

"At first?" asked Lambi.

"Aye. You have been made a slave, but you need not remain one forever!" sniffed the Vaeringi, "Your value is set around four thousand silver *miliaresia*. If you earn that much, you can buy your freedom. You can still fight in the arena after that, of course, but it would be your choice."

The woman named Calluna seemed displeased that Lambi was chattering with her colleague in the barbarian language of the North, and barked something in her strange southern language at the Vaeringi. He responded, and she laughed again. They prepared to move on to evaluate the rest of the slaves in the lot, but Lambi was not ready to be ignored just yet.

"*She* is going to train *me*?" Lambi laughed, real laughter, for the first time since he had been enslaved. "I mean, I can see she's got some meat and muscle on her bones, but she's so *short*! And, I mean, she only has one hand! You have got to be joking . . ." He trailed off as he saw the Vaeringi's face go even paler than it was before, and apparently muttering some kind of translation at Calluna's command.

Calluna stepped forward and looked up into Lambi's eyes. There was no trace of emotion on her face. None. Lambi felt a chill crawl up his spine. She said something in Palnorrani, her voice tranquil and devoid of passion. Lambi felt the chill deepen. She did not look at the Vaeringi, but she must have been telling him to translate, because he cleared his throat nervously and then stepped up behind her. "She says . . . she says that she will . . . she will show you something. Right here and now."

Lambi laughed again, but he was beginning to get a bit of a chill staring into Calluna's dark, expressionless eyes. "Well, if you want to take these chains off, that is fine," he said, thrusting his manacles forward, "but I do not know if I have it in me to fight a one-handed woman!"

Another, younger *lanista* stepped forward with a heavy brass ring of keys and began unlocking the manacles around Lambi's wrists and ankles, muttering all the while in Palnorrani. While he worked on the locks, Calluna spoke again, and the interpreter relayed, "Uh . . . she says that if you survive, she may have to re-evaluate whether or not you'll have any value as a gladiator. She thinks . . . um . . . she thinks you might be too . . . too *stupid* to make a good gladiator . . . um . . . oh dear . . ."

Lambi refused to take the bait, still laughing as the young man unchained him. "She talks tough, I'll give her that! Now, how does she want to . . .?"

There was a sudden clatter as the chains fell away and hit the ground at Lambi's feat. The young *lanista* with the keys hurled himself to one side, as if terrified. Lambi thought the fellow was afraid to be around an unchained barbarian, but suddenly Calluna struck out at him, a flurry of kicks and punches he had not been expecting. He took some painful blows that might have crippled a lesser man, but as it was he staggered back in surprise and began to try to block the assault. The problem was, she seemed to anticipate every move he made. She was everywhere, moving with a lithe grace and ferocity that startled Lambi, and which proved impossible to resist effectively. He held out for a few heartbeats, then was struck in the groin, punched in the throat with the stump of her right arm, kicked in the knees so that his lefts were swept out from under him, and he was left gasping and kneeling on the ground, choking and trying to recover himself. Calluna stood over him imperiously, with only a slight, cold smirk giving any expression to her features, as the other *lanista* chained Lambi's wrists and ankles again.

Lambi was still gasping and coughing when he realized that Calluna and the other *lanistae* had moved on again. The Vaeringi was still standing over him. "You will make a fine gladiator, I am certain," said the interpreter, "but you must learn not to trifle with Calluna Scaevola. She can end you with one hand. She almost did."

Lambi scowled up at the Vaeringi, feeling his face grow hot with embarrassment. "Scaevola?" he asked, " Is that her tribe or clan? Did she lose the other hand in a gladiatorial match, or on the battlefield? She seems fierce enough to be a gladiatrix or a soldier!"

The Vaeringi shook his head. "She *was* a gladiatrix, but she didn't *lose* that hand. She was born without it. Her family figured a handless girl would be a burden and sold her to the factions; they probably thought they were selling her as fodder for the beasts. But she had spirit, and the Brotherhood of the Sand is very good at recognizing spirit. She learned to fight; she knew she had to be at least twice as good as opponents who had twice her number of hands. She has no family now but the Purple Faction of the Brotherhood of the Sand. No clan, no tribe. Her surname, Scaevola, is an ancient one in the Norrani language. In their language, it means 'Lefty'."

***

Lambi had done well. His natural size and strength were honed into a fighting edge by Calluna. At first he hated her - hated her arrogance, hated that she was stronger and faster than he was, hated that she could beat him any time she wanted to. He hated how hard she made him work, and that her training was emblematic of his enslavement. He hated having to learn the brain-twisting Palnorrani language in order to communicate.

As weeks slid into months, his hatred began to soften, to turn into something more akin to admiration. It had been Lambi's understanding that the women of the south were soft and coddled. Maybe the majority of them were; there were very few "sisters" in the Brotherhood. But Calluna Scaevola was as fierce as any Northern shieldmaiden. Fiercer than many, he was forced to admit. And she was beautiful. He found he was ashamed of how grateful he was when she took him to her bed.

The Purple Faction owned them both. Calluna was not bothered by this; she had been a slave for as long as she could remember. She did not understand Lambi's obsession with obtaining his freedom. On his first day in Mikligardhur, that Vaeringi had told him that his value was set at four thousand *miliaresia*. A little less than fifty marks in Northern currency. A fortune. And as slaves, they were not paid. But under Palnorran law, slaves could keep a *peculium* - a fund of their own money with which to buy their freedom. And gladiators did receive gifts from fans and admirers, tokens from their adoring public. The better the performance, the more entertained the crowd was, the more money was showered upon the gladiators on the sands. And so Lambi had begun to save his money against the day when he could buy his freedom.

Lambi was popular. He was exotic, a fair-haired Northerner whose pale skin bronzed under the pitiless Palnorran sun. His blonde hair and beard grew long, like a mane, and he was nicknamed "Lion of the Arena." That always made Lambi smile, for he remembered that they day they had met, Calluna had hoped that he would be more lion than lamb. As his list of victories grew, Lambi drew larger and larger crowds. He gained celebrity. He did not really understand the strange ways of the south, in which an enslaved entertainer could be popular and famous. But he knew he still resented these people with their wicked, decadent blood sports and their patent dedication to vice of every kind.

Lambi's growing fame as a gladiator did not bother him. Let the corrupt folk of the south adore him if they would! It meant he received larger and larger donations from his vile fans. Most successful gladiators spent their winnings, on food or drink or slaves of their own, living the high life while remaining slaves themselves. It was actually expected for successful slaves to become as self-indulgent as their masters in this mad city. Lambi's ascetic lifestyle embarrassed some Sandmen, who were ashamed to see him living such a simple existence while they revelled in their own vices and debauchery. But they did not emulate him.

Calluna's affection for Lambi faded somewhat as the months turned into years, though it never disappeared entirely. They ceased to be lovers, finding other fellow-slaves to share their beds, but they remained colleagues of a sort (though Lambi was ever the junior partner in any work they did together). They trained gladiators for the Brotherhood; Lambi found himself interpreting for Calluna as that Vaeringi had done when Lambi was first dragged to the arena in chains. Calluna said that it should cheer him to have come so far. So many gladiators who had started as he had, barbarians brought to Mikligardhur in chains, did not survive their first few weeks of the Brotherhood's rigorous training and first real fighting matches. But Lambi was a survivor. He had no idea of ending up in a grave in the catacombs under the arena. Ultimately, that was the fate of almost every gladiator in the so-called Silver City.

***

It had taken him years, and it felt longer to Lambi than even that span, but he had managed to assemble a small fortune. His victories in the Grand Arena brought him fame, of course; the Lion of the Arena was one of the most celebrated figures in Mikligardhur's sporting circuit. But the gifts and money that came from admiring fans and patrons - it had started as just a trickle of coins, and the flow had steadily increased over the years into a torrent of riches - had poured into his *peculium* until at last, Lambi felt he was ready. He had acquired the equivalent of four thousand *miliaresia* some time ago, but now he had almost double that figure. Enough to both purchase his freedom and live comfortably, as well as provide for new weapons and gear (his own kit had been taken from him long ago, when he had first been taken prisoner by the Palnorran Legions.

With confidence and pride, Lambi had asked for a meeting with higher representatives of the Purple Faction, which still held the title to him as a slave. He had smiled the whole way to that meeting, feeling as if he were floating on air. He came up from the catacombs under the arena and walked across the sands to the offices of the Purple Faction, actually enjoying the feel of the sand shifting under his sandals and giddy with the notion that soon it would be for the last time. Freedom! In the North, freedom was a sacred thing. His enslavement had been an abomination. The end of this horror brought him joy that welled up like a fountain in his soul.

He entered the well-lit meeting chamber, with its high windows and vaulted ceiling. The room was designed to give the place an open, spacious feeling that Lambi felt contrasted with the dark, cramped conditions under the arena where the majority of the slaves of the sporting factions dwelt. A light breeze flowed through the windows and stirred the air. Of course the meeting room was pleasant - sometimes senators or even the emperor himself came down to meet with the heads of the Purple Faction! Lambi had learned that anything with which a member of the privileged classes of Palnorran society might come into contact in any way was always better, cleaner, and more comfortable than what the majority had to endure. Not that kings and jarls in the North did not also live better than their common freefolk, but the thing that disturbed Lambi was that the gap between them seemed so much wider and deeper, here, a vast canyon between rich and poor, free (if any Southerner could be said to be truly free) and slave.

The only furnishings of this bright, airy room were a beautiful citruswood table and a set of comfortable-looking chairs. Lambi did not sit, but stared out the window at the city streets. He could smell the salt air of the sea his people called the Midhjardhurhaf on the breeze. *Perhaps I can find a Vaeringjar ship heading back to the North, when this is over*, he thought.

The others came into the room behind him. Grim-looking old men of the Faction, wearing their ceremonial togas for an official meeting, hot and uncomfortable wrapped up in so many pounds of wool. The scent of perfumes drifted with them, exotic and strange in Lambi's nostrils. Among the scents, he could also detect the odor of the addictive narcotic called silver lotus, a widespread vice among Palnorrans and their slaves. Lambi felt his lip curl in sneering contempt for the ways of these people. Still, he did not turn to look at them.

It was protocol to have a gladiator or gladiatrix bodyguard present for the faction representatives during any such meeting, and Lambi knew even before he turned around that they had brought Calluna Scaevola. He wasn't even sure how he knew - was it a scent she wore? Did he know the tread of her feet and the rhythm of her gait so well? Or did he just assume that the would bring *her*, of all the possible guards, just to rattle him, keep him off-balance. And of course, there could be more innocent reasons for choosing Calluna.

After all, she had been Lambi's *lanista*. Was it not fitting that she be present for any discussion of his future as a slave and a gladiator?

Lambi turned to see the grumpy old men of the faction scowling, and behind them, Calluna Scaevola leaning against the wall by the door. She wore a *gladius* at her waist, and a slight smirk on her face. The men carefully arranged the folds of their garments as they seated themselves. Lambi chose to ignore their hostile countenances. Let them stew in their anger, so long as they let him go!

"I suppose that you know why I called for this meeting," Lambi began, trying to keep his voice even. He just hoped he could keep his Palnorrani grammar straight.

"Nay, we do not!" barked the most wrinkled and miserable-looking representative of the Faction. "Nor do we enjoy being summoned frivolously, barbarian! So you had better get on with it, and the reason had better be good!"

"Well," said Lambi, clearing his throat, "As you know, I have been a gladiator for many years now. I have been quite successful, and I have made a lot of money for the faction, and for myself. But I feel that it is time for me to return to my homeland and my people! I have the four thousand *miliaresia* that the Purple Faction demanded as the price of my freedom. I want to . . . *buy* myself! Draw up your papers, and let us be about the business of getting my freedom!"

Lambi was surprised to see the corners of their mouths turn up slightly, as if *amused.* They did not seem surprised, nor angry, that he intended to leave. They were *smiling.* One of them leaned forward in his chair across the table and said simply, "No."

Lambi was taken aback by this. "I have the money . . .," he began.

"Oh, we are certain that you do," said the one who seemed to be their spokesman, moving his hand as if to wave away an unpleasant thought, "You *are* quite successful, as you said, and however much money you have brought the faction, you surely got more than a few personal gifts. And the 'Lion of the Arena' *does* have quite a reputation for ascetic living, so we assume you have been hoarding your silver. All of that is well and good. But you do not yet have enough silver to purchase your freedom, I'm afraid."

Lambi snarled. "I have the four thousand, and more," he growled

"Four thousand *miliaresia* . . . where did you get that figure? That's what a beginning gladiator with a little training, a little skill, and a bit of luck will fetch. You, slave, are more valuable. You've survived years on the sands. You've filled our coffers, and if you remain, you will bring even more silver to our faction. You're too valuable an investment, fool! Four thousand? When you began, aye! But now? Now you're worth . . . let us see . . . at least thirteen thousand *miliaresia*. That's a good price for a middle-rank gladiator of your experience, training, and skill. If you can give us thirteen thousand, we should be glad to draw up papers of manumission and see you on your way!"

Lambi growled again. Calluna was trying to look casual, but with his peripheral vision he saw he adjust her stance, every muscle poised for combat, and her only hand come to rest on the hilt of the *gladius*. These stupid men did not realize that even unarmed, Lambi could kill them all, and without much effort. But Calluna knew, and she wanted him to know that she could not allow that.

"That . . . that isn't *fair*," Lambi finally managed to grind out through gritted teeth, "It took me years to acquire what I have! Even at the rate I get now, it will take many more years to pay that!" In the silence that followed this outburst, Lambi could see the men trying to conceal their glee at his distress. They *knew* this would happen. It was deliberate! "I see," he said, after a moment, "and by the time I make thirteen hundred, if I survive, I'll be an even more famous and valuable gladiator, and the price will have gone up yet again. Until there is no way for you vultures to profit from me any further, the price will always be higher. By then, I'm likely to be buried in the catacombs under the arena. One way or another. That's it, isn't it?"

The spokesman did not bother hide his smile. "Although your accent is barbarous and your grasp of our tongue atrocious, I see that you understand. You might as well spend some of your silver. Get yourself a girl, some wine, some silver lotus! Live a little, slave, before you end up, as you say, under the arena!"

Lambi stood up. He towered over these miserable, stunted Southerners. Calluna tensed even more, if that were possible. He glowered for a minute, then stalked towards the door.

The spokesman chuckled. "That would seem to conclude our business," he muttered.

Calluna made no move to stop him, but as Lambi passed her, she whispered, "Where are you going?"

Without looking at her, Lambi answered, "I am going to take the man's advice. I am going to live a little. I am going to the Last Taste for a cup of wine."

Calluna let him go. She would catch up with him at the Last Taste after she had conferred with the leadership of the Purple Faction. She was certain that Lambi was going to try to run.

***

Lambi had decided to run, but he knew he had to be smart about it. As far as the law was concerned, he was still the property of the Purple Faction of the Brotherhood of the Sand. He was also a celebrity, which meant that people recognized him when he went out on the street. He would not get very far without being identified, and word being sent to his masters. He could not count on other Sandmen to help, either - Lambi had discovered that one surprisingly insidious aspect of slavery in the South was that its rules were enforced by the slaves themselves. If other Sandmen knew he was planning to run, to cheat the system, they would cheerfully hunt him down and kill him themselves. Lambi could only pray that Calluna Scaevola had not told anyone of her suspicions. He suspected that rumor had not spread among the Sandmen, or he would have heard of it, but he guessed that she did have permission from the faction leadership to terminate him if he ran.

Lambi headed up through the Grand Arena to the streets of the city. He could hear people call his name and point him out to their companions - "Lion of the Arena!" - as he passed, but he ignored it. He went straight to a business owned by House Gabras, and presented his documents that certified the money he had on deposit there. He had not dared to keep his almost eight thousand *miliaresia* in his quarters under the arena, or on his person, before now. He proceeded to withdraw his money, but in the more portable form of some pre-selected gemstones and a pouch full of gold *imperatores*. The gold coins were worth more, and allowed him to carry the equivalent of thousands of silver coins on his belt. Of course, for the keeping of the money, changing the money, and the discretion, House Gabras took a sizeable cut of Lambi's money for themselves, but Lambi did not care too much. He had expected to spend half of it to buy his freedom; he was therefore perfectly willing to spend a much smaller percentage while planning to escape his slavery without paying for it.

It felt odd walking through the city with a fortune on his belt. Lambi remained especially vigilant against pickpockets on his way back to the Grand Arena. Once there, he quickly descended once more into the warren of tunnels under the arena. He stealthily crept into an armory and stole some weapons. Slaves were not supposed to be armed except during practice or a gladiatorial match, but no one ever dared to break those rules, so no one really kept watch on the armories. He wrapped the *gladii* in an old cloak and carried them down one series of stairs after another into the catacombs below. He stashed the cloak containing the swords and his pouch containing his fortune in a burial niche that he could find again, then went back to his quarters and collapsed on his pallet to sleep.

Lambi slept fitfully that night, dreaming of his homeland. At one point he woke up and was aware of someone else in the room with him. He knew it was Calluna Scaevola. She was checking in on him. She was quiet; she didn't want to wake him, so he pretended to sleep. She quietly knelt down and sifted silently through a small pile of his possessions. The room had no lighting of its own; the only light shone dimly from a torch in the corridor outside the room. Once she was satisfied he wasn't making a break for it in the middle of the night or concealing an arsenal in his room, she crept away. He heard her whisper, "Damn you, Lambi, don't do it. Don't run."

But Lambi knew he had to run.

Lambi had a fight scheduled for the early afternoon the next day.

He ate breakfast, he went to training, he talked to his fellow Sandmen about the match - trying to act as normal as possible. It made sense that a gladiator who wanted to try to run would do so before a match, so as to avoid being killed in the fight. The few gladiators who did run usually did so to avoid a match. This was an act of cowardice that Palnorran society could never forgive, and a contravention of the *sacramentum gladiatorium* - the gladiatorial oath - in which they swore in Norrani to endure "*uri, vinciri, verberari ferroque necari*" - "to be burned, bound, beaten, and slain by the sword" if that was the will of the gods and the *editor* of the games (and honestly, the gladiators were encouraged to think of the *editor* of the games *as* their god). Runaway gladiators were almost always trying to avoid fulfilling their oath.

Lambi was not worried about the match, and was not trying to avoid fulfilling his oath because of cowardice. In fact, he intended to keep his oath and his appointment in the arena. He knew that the faction and the Brotherhood would see him as an oathbreaker whenever he fled, unless he were lawfully released from bondage, but though it pained Lambi, he did not see any way to do that. They had no intention of keeping their word, of letting him go, they simply intended to keep moving the goalpost farther and farther away. He had tried to play by the rules, but if his masters felt free to break them at will, Lambi had to be prepared to do so as well. Otherwise he would remain a slave for the rest of his life.

Afternoon approached, and while Lambi knew he was being

watched, he did not mind. He focused on training for the match, stretching his muscles and practicing his moves. He had spotted Calluna Scaevola watching him, trying to remain unobserved as she did so. She would expect him to run before the match, so he would run after. She would expect him to be unarmed and unprepared, so he made sure his cache of weapons and supplies in the catacombs was ready, adding some food and drink to the swords and money he had stashed there. Lambi knew that his best chance for survival was to do what was least expected.

***

The morning shows were the cheap ones. Execution of criminals by beast or by gladiator, hunts of less exotic animals, that sort of thing. The afternoon was when the *real* matches were scheduled. Lambi was paired off against an Omurian called Juba. Juba favored light armor and spear-like weapons. Juba was fast; his speed reminded Lambi of Calluna. The Lion of the Arena took to the sands and faced the dark-skinned, exotic Juba. The crowds were beginning to call Juba the "Young Lion". It was said that there were lions in Omuria.

Lambi liked Juba, as much as he liked anyone in this accursed city, and he thought the Young Lion had spirit and potential. He did not really want to kill Juba, but he did not intend to lose this match, either. Lambi summoned all of his reserves of energy, and as he took to the sands, he fell upon Juba like a thunderbolt, charging him, forcing the young man to stay on the defensive as the Northerner struck again and again and again! When Juba tried to raise his spears to drive Lambi back or regain the offensive, Lambi lashed out at the wooden shafts of the weapons with all his might, shattering Juba's weapons. Lambi knew the young man would still be dangerous, armed with just the broken spear-shafts or even completely unarmed, so he kept coming, relentless as an avalanche, until he could force Juba down to the sand. Holding razor-sharp swords at Juba's throat, he waited. By all rights, Lambi certainly could have slain the Omurian. But he wanted to give Juba a chance to surrender, despite the shame and loss of status the Young Lion would suffer if he did. But Lambi was determined to escape his bondage, and if that meant shaming a brother gladiator, well, he was sorry, but he would do it.

At last Juba gave the signal, begging for mercy. Lambi let out a breath that he had not realized he had been holding, waiting to see if Juba would choose to die or was willing to lower himself in the eyes of the Brotherhood by asking quarter. Lambi's eyes flicked to the *editor* of the games. The *editor* hesitated, frowned, and finally gave the signal, thumb down, that indicated Lambi should ground his weapons and spare the young Omurian's life. With a sigh, Lambi dropped his swords to the sand and walked off to the thunderous applause of the crowd.

As soon as he was out of public view, Lambi began to run, dashing down stairs and jogging through narrow tunnels. Any Sandmen who saw him would assume that he was heading to his quarters, but he sped past them and down farther into the catacombs. He found the burial niches where his gear was stowed and quickly donned the swordbelt with its *gladii* and the pouch of riches. His pack contained a waterskin and rations. He would head to the docks and try to stow away in the hold of a ship, preferably a ship heading back to the North. This would work. It had to.

Lambi started to head down the tunnel that led to the beast pens. Those areas were the least well-guarded, and if he hoped to avoid being seen, that was his best bet. But as he turned down a passageway towards the beasts, a shadow stepped out of an intersecting tunnel into his path. It was Calluna Scaevola. Of course.

"No one has to know about this," she hissed, "if you turn back now. Turn back, return the swords to the armory, and go to bed. No one will ever know you tried to break your oath. I swear it!"

"I have worked for years to buy my freedom," Lambi answered calmly, "and I learned that they have no intention of ever letting me go. I'm too valuable to ever let me go. Some slaves in this accursed city may be allowed to buy their freedom, but they will never let *me* do it! I do not intend to be buried here, under the arena. I *shall* breathe the free air of the North again! Unless you stop me . . ."

"I don't want to kill you," Calluna said sadly. "I don't know if I ever loved you, really, but I know I care for you, and I don't want to kill you."

"You are going to have to," replied Lambi, "or get out of my way. Or force me to kill you, Scaevola."

A scowl of annoyance crossed Calluna's features. "Don't call me that, Lambi. Put down the swords and let's talk."

Lambi shifted to a fighting stance and hefted the twin blades in his hands. "Nay. I am done with talking. Get out of my way, or we fight! If I kill you, I'll bury you in the catacombs before I leave, and put a couple of gold *imperatores* on your eyes. I know you Southern folk are superstitious! But if you kill me . . . just . . . just promise me that you won't bury me here. Not under the arena! Burn my body on a pyre by the seashore, if you would do me honor!"

"Lambi, I can't let you go . . .," began Calluna.

"Then one of us dies here today," growled Lambi. "Now . . . are we going to fight?"

Calluna hesitated. For a moment, Lambi thought she really might do it. Then he saw that her hesitation was more than just a moment of weakness. She stepped back and lowered her blade. "You won't reconsider?" she asked.

"Nay. I was born a free man, and I must die a free man in a free country if I can, Calluna. Please tell me you understand. Please?"

Lambi was surprised to hear his voice quaver.

She shook her head but gestured with the stump of her right arm to the intersecting tunnel from which she had come. "I will never understand you, barbarian! You should go that way. I understand why you thought the animal pens were the safest way out, but you would still have to get out through the Grand Arena. If you go that way, you'll find a place where the catacombs connect to the city sewers. Follow the way the water flows and eventually it empties into the sea. It's a way out of the city without having to worry about running into patrols."

"Why are you letting me go?" Lambi asked.

"I don't really know. Maybe it is what we shared, when I took you to my bed. Maybe I still think of you fondly. Mostly, I think, it is because you don't belong here. This is my world, under the arena. More so than in the arena itself. The Brotherhood is made up of my brothers. And my sisters. But you were never really one of us, were you? You don't belong under the arena. Not in my bed. Not in my barracks. Not in a grave. You don't belong in my world under the arena. Go back to your world, and leave me to mine!"

Lambi blinked back tears that surprised him. Why was he crying? He knew she was right. This was what he had wanted. But he had cared for Calluna, for the woman who had trained him under the arena to fight on its sands above. He knew that leaving meant truly severing this life from all other, all of Midhgardhur and the world under the arena. "Farewell!" he whispered, and began to jog down the tunnel Calluna had indicated. If she were correct and telling the truth, it would lead him out the the city. Once out, no one could tell him from any other Vaeringi, and he could find a ship heading north. He would never again see her world, the world under the arena.

8. SPRING SACRIFICE

The folk of Rorvik knew that springtime was at hand because the light of the dawning sun touched the sacred standing stones in just the right way, at just the right angles, and every morning the golden rays crept closer and closer to perfect alignment with the Stone of Spring. This was the Old Way. Not too many folk in the simple fishing village put any stock in the calendars developed in the last few centuries that aped the reckoning of the fallen Norrani Imperium of the south; and everyone knew that the weather was not to be trusted as a guide. On the island of Sjaelland, winter weather could linger long into spring, and the winds that blew in off the sea could carry illusions of warmer or cooler weather from day to day. Nay, the only true guide was the Old Way and the standing stones, as the gods called the Vanir had long ago decreed.

The vernal equinox was still a few days away when the killings began. In a small village like Rorvik, even a single death is a notable event, so when a fisherman named Kjotvi was found floating face-down in the shallow bay among the reeds that gave the village its name (for Rorvik was said to come from the words "Reed Bay" in the Thjodhiskmal tongue of the North), folk paid attention. Anlaf, the alderman of the village, was summoned immediately. He investigated, but there was no sign of weapon-hurt upon the corpse of poor Kjotvi, and so it was the official opinion that he had drowned, whether through drunken carelessness (for Kjotvi was known to drink a great deal more than he ought!) or through the agency some terror rising from the deep (for there are surely monsters who dwell in the depths of the Northern seas, and some of them do venture quite close to land on occasion). The matter would have rested there, had not another body been found the next day near the reedy shallows where Kjotvi's lifeless body had been found.

This second body was that of Mother Sigurlaug, as she was known, an old herb-wife and *spaekona*, or seeress, who lived on the edge of the forest. She frequently made lonely forays into the woods to collect herbs and mushrooms and other ingredients, whether for her remedies or for her stewpot, or possibly both, none could say. Everyone called her "Mother" Sigurlaug, for she had aided in the birthing of many of the folk in Rorvik, and she was beloved as a gentle, matronly figure, despite her potentially sinister gifts as a practitioner of *spae* magic. Uncanny she might have been, but she was loved and trusted by almost all in the village. When a young girl set out for the forest to see if the first flowers of the season were blooming yet, she found Mother Sigurlaug's body on the path by the bay, the one that led to the glade of the standing stones. She ran back to the village screaming, and thus notified her parents, who then went to the alderman for help.

Anlaf dutifully investigated the second death in two days. He felt the creeping chill of certainty, certainty that this was not just a coincidence, crawl and settle over him like a cold mist. Life was hard throughout the North, and winters brutal. Although the official end of winter was days away, Anlaf knew that the weather alone could be lethal well into spring, and that (unfortunately) the weather was not the only threat. Sometimes, the terrible winters would drive starving beasts from the forests into places they normally avoided, like the places where humans dwelt, to attack the very young or very old, or if desperate enough, to attack anyone at all. But Rorvik was so small, so isolated, that two deaths in two days was unthinkable to most of the villagers. Virtually unheard of! Anlaf took the path along the bay that led to the forest until he came to where Mother Sigurlaug's corpse rested.

As with Kjotvi, there was no sign that weapons had been used against Mother Sigurlaug. But her neck had been broken, twisted at an unnatural angle, and that spoke of murder. It was not an accident; Sigurlaug had not simply stumbled and twisted her head around. It was not possible. Nor was she a drunk like Kjotvi, who had been a careless fool probably doomed to get himself killed eventually no matter what else fate might hold. She was a steady and sober woman. Nor could Anlaf even imagine that it were an animal attack. Fish had been feeding on Kjotvi, so Anlaf was not sure that some sea creature had not slain him in the first place, but Mother Sigurlaug's body was on land, and dry. She was not killed by a sea monster. And any animal on land that might have been hungry enough to attack her, say a wolf or bear, would have eaten her flesh. Aside from the broken neck, she seemed to be intact. And that indicated murder. But who would want to harm Mother Sigurlaug, or even that harmless old drunk Kjotvi for that matter?

Anlaf examined the area carefully. There was an odd stench in the air, like the foulness of the muck at the bottom of a mire, or the brackish, silty ooze of the nearby salt marshes. But Anlaf could find nothing to account for the smell, except some odd slimy goo on Sigurlaug's clothing. Anlaf was not certain whence the slimy residue had come, but it could have been a consequence of wandering around in the wilderness, with nothing to do with the death at all. Or it might have been a significant clue. Anlaf had no way to know which.

Anlaf went back to the village and found Arndis Siggadottir, a girl of about fourteen winters who sometimes acted as courier for the isolated settlement. Arndis had a nose like a hawk's beak, a face spangled with freckles, and a fierce disposition. When she rode as courier, she always went fully armed - a chainmail byrnie, spear, sword, and bow, with a quiver full of arrows of all sorts, for hunting and for war. "Get your gear," he told the girl, who was out helping her mother with laundry.

Arndis looked to her mother, Erna, but Erna merely nodded and said, "Better do as the alderman says, child!" So. Word had spread of the second death. Erna had been expecting this.

Arndis ducked into the low house she still shared with her parents, and emerged a few moments later with her chain byrnie thrown over her clothing and her bundle of weapons. The girl had been collecting arms for years; she might, in fact, have the best array of weapons and armor in the whole village. What Arndis took with her on any given ride was only a fraction of the girl's armory. She began to adjust her gear as she followed Anlaf away from her her parents' house, towards the stables. "What word would you have me bring to the court?" she asked the alderman gravely.

Anlaf sighed. He was feeling old. Arndis was the same age as his own daughter, Oddlaf. Every year, they seemed more and more to become young women rather than young girls (which was still how he usually thought of them), and every year his hair grew grayer and his joints ached more. How had he become so old? He realized that he had become distracted - another sign of his age? -

and sighed again. "I need you to ride to the Hjartarholl at Hleidhra, and tell the folk at the royal court that we've had two deaths in two days we cannot account for. Tell them that I am investigating. The king may want to send his own men to look into it, or he might decide that we can handle it on our own, but it is our duty to report it, so you are carrying my report to the court on behalf of the village. Understand?"

Arndis nodded, freckled face still grave, and said, "Aye, sir. Any reason to expect trouble?" Her hands clenched her weapons reflexively. Anlaf wondered idly what "trouble" the lass was imagining.

Anlaf hesitated a moment before he answered the girl. "Both deaths happened near the edge of the forest and the bay. You'll be heading the opposite direction, so if there is something . . . Well, you should be safe enough. But it was a hard winter, and spring is not yet fully come. The wilderness between here and Hleidhra may indeed be perilous. Be careful."

Arndis grinned fiercely. "Aye, sir! Last spring, on a run to Hleidhra, a pack of starving wolves came after me and Vaengfotur! I killed them all, you know! I went back later and skinned them, and made a nice wolf-fur cloak for my father!" Vaengfotur, whose name meant "Wing-foot," was the horse that the village maintained, at public expense, for just such occasions as the need to send someone to contact the royal court swiftly. The incident with the wolves was a well-known story in Rorvik; Arndis' father Siggi loved to show off his fur-lined cloak around the village.

Anlaf nodded, but replied, "I know you can look after yourself, girl! Just be extra careful this time, all right?" Every time he sent a rider to court, he worried. The villagers were his responsibility, and how could he watch over them when they rode away from the village? On an errand for *him*, no less. He would be doubly responsible for anything that happened to a courier.

"I shall, sir! I promise!" Arndis checked her saddle and saddlebags, making certain she had all she would need for the journey. Sjaelland was not a vast country, but it was still about a hundred miles from Rorvik to the royal court at Hleidra. It would take a few days, longer if it snowed again, and it would not do to find oneself ill-provisioned in the wild, open countryside. "Oh," continued Arndis, sounding embarrassed, "I was supposed to spend some time with Oddlaf over the next few days! Can you give her my apologies?"

"I shall tell my daughter, fear not. She knows that what you do is important for the safety of our village! Go!" Anlaf smiled to himself. Oddlaf had been friends with Arndis all her life. He thought his daughter envied her fierce friend, sometimes. But Oddlaf preferred a quiet life, and Anlaf could not help but be a little thankful for that. He wanted his daughter to be safe. But he would be heartbroken if anything happened to Arndis, too. He sighed yet again as Arndis led

Vaengfotur out of the stable and climbed into the saddle.

"I shall return as soon as I can," Arndis promised. She began to guide Vaengfotur towards the northern end of the village, where the trail to Hleidhra began. Anlaf watched her go, then turned his mind back to the problem at hand. Was someone in the village murdering fellow villagers? Was there an outlaw lurking in the woods, driven mad by exile in winter and taking out his frustration on Rorvik for some reason? What was going on?

Anlaf went next to the longhouse that served as communal meeting place for the folk of Rorvik. His daughter Oddlaf helped to maintain the hall, and he wanted to tell her that Arndis had gone to Hleidhra, but he had other, more pressing reasons to visit the longhouse. In a town so small that it lacked even a true tavern, the common hall was a meeting place where one could get a drink, take a break from one's labors, relax, and meet with other villagers. It was the next best thing to a tavern.

As Anlaf entered the hall, he was surprised by the size of the crowd gathered there. It seemed as if a quarter of the village's tiny population was in the hall. There was a man's voice loudly speaking above the mutters of the gathered folk. Hugaldur Freysgodhi was addressing the crowd.

Hugaldur was an odd fellow. He had come from another village near Hleidhra a decade back or so, a wandering cleric of Freyur, the god of fertility and agriculture. Hugaldur had settled down here because there were villagers who made their living by farming rather than fishing, and they had asked him to stay to bless their livestock and their crops. He had a small farm of his own on the north end of the village now, but many in the village still thought of him as an outsider because he had not been born in Rorvik. Nevertheless, Hugaldur had made Rorvik his home, and was fiercely protective of his adopted home and its folk.

But why was Hugaldur holding forth in the longhouse now? It was not one of the regular times or places for Hugaldur's preaching. But as Anlaf listened, his frown deepened.

"I say to you, you are *wrong!* What you suggest is not right! Why would you even consider such a horror?" Hugaldur sounded desperate. "You suggest that the gods are demanding *human* sacrifice? Why, for the love of Freyur? WHY?"

"Because we remember the old stories," replied Kolbrun, a flinty-eyed old fishwife, "because it was part of the Old Ways, sometimes. We no longer make that kind of offering to the gods, and look what has come! *Something* killed Kjotvi, *something* killed Sigurlaug, and now the first day of spring is just days away! When the morning sunlight touches the Stone of Spring, it must have the blood of our sacrifice upon it, else spring may never come to us and our village may die! The gods already kill us, one by one!"

"You speak of the Jotnar, not the Vanir," cried Hugaldur, "the wicked gods of the giants, the raw elemental powers of nature that seek only to destroy mankind! The Vanir are our allies *against* such evil; we must not offend them by siding with our own enemies!"

"Might as well give it up, Hugi," called an old farmer named Vefastur, using the priest's nickname, "We remember the old stories, the old rites, the Old Ways! You've been offering up prayers to Freyur for the turning of spring, but the winter weather lingers! Our people are being taken! But *we* can make an offering to turn this evil from us!"

"By committing an even greater evil, Vefastur?" asked Hugaldur, "Who blessed your crops and flocks last spring?"

"You did," spat Vefastur, looking a little shamefaced. "But -"

"It was *not* I who blessed you, Vesfastur!" shouted Hugaldur, "Oh, I offered the prayers, but it was Lord Freyur who made your crops grow, Lord Freyur who made your flocks increase! Do you think he will not do so again? How would the Jotnar, the Lords of Ice and Fire, bring aught but suffering and disaster to you?"

"A man doesn't turn to the Jotnar to bless his farm," said Vefastur stubbornly, though he had the decency to look ashamed, still. "But if the Jotnar have turned their eyes upon him, a man can make offering that they might pass over him and his home without destroying him!"

"This is insane!" whispered Anlaf to himself. He spoke softly, to himself, so he was surprised to hear a familiar voice whisper, "Aye, it is!" He jumped a little and turned to see his only daughter, Oddlaf, standing behind him.

Oddlaf gave her father a quick smile of greeting, but then her face turned grave. "I don't know how it started," she whispered, "One moment, our folk were gathered for a drink, discussing the bad news - I heard what happened to poor Mother Sigurlaug! - and the next thing, some of the old-timers were talking about how in ancient days, when something like this happened, they would make a spring sacrifice - a *human* sacrifice - to the Jotnar to avert disaster. Some of them were getting pretty riled up, discussing *who* among us would make a good sacrifice, and then Hugaldur arrived, and now . . ."

"Aye, I see," said Anlaf, "I'm going to try to put a stop to this! Neighbor turned against neighbor, good folk of our village talking about *appeasing* the Lords of Ice and Fire! That's horrible! I've already sent Arndis to Hleidhra to notify the king's court of these killings. But by the time the king sends help - *if* he sends any help - it will already be spring, and these fools will have murdered one of their neighbors if I let them!"

Oddlaf nodded. "Aye, father! But how -"

"I shall have to think of something," said Anlaf, "But never mind that, right now! I want you to go home now, and bar the door to the house once you're there! There's no telling how ugly this will get!"

"But father -," began Oddlaf.

"Do as I say, daughter!" hissed the alderman, and he held open the door so that she could scurry out. Then he turned back to look at the gathered crowd, which was still engaged in heated debate about the old rites of spring sacrifice, and whether or not the villagers could countenance ancient rites to placate the Jotnar as well as those to honor the Aesir and Vanir.

With his left hand, Anlaf slammed the door shut, startling the other villagers in the longhouse. Shaggy heads whipped around to face the alderman. With his right hand, he drew his longsword. Very few folk in the village had such a fine weapon as Anlaf's sword. In the North, every free person is expected to be able to defend themselves and their families, and serve their king in battle if need be, but few of the villagers here owned more than a rusty old spear and a dagger. Anlaf had been given his sword by the Skjoldung king himself at Hjartarholl, the center of royal power on the island of Sjaelland. He held up that sword now, the gleaming steel that was his badge of office as alderman of the village. He took care with this blade; it was well-oiled and polished.

"SILENCE!" roared Anlaf, and between the surprise at the slamming door and the sight of him holding bare steel, he got it. The villagers gaped at him.

"There has been at least one murder in this village, probably two!" shouted Anlaf, "We shall *not* add to the list by murdering one of our own as a sacrifice!"

"I heard they weren't *murdered*," rasped Kolbrun the fishwife, "I heard they were *taken*! Taken by the spirits of sea and stone! Taken to appease the Lords of Ice and Fire!"

"I said *silence!* I've sent to Hjartarholl to seek the king's help, but until his help arrives, *I* speak for the king in this village," boomed Anlaf, "and we will have *order* here! Not chaos!" He pounded the pommel of his shining, polished sword down on a wooden tabletop for emphasis. Several of the villagers jumped in surprise. *Good. If I can surprise them, I can seize the advantage.* "You heard Hugaldur! He is the *godhi* of Freyur! If you seek answers from the divine, *he* has given them! Not the forbidden gods, the Jotnar, Lords of Ice and Fire! They care for us about as much as a howling blizzard or a raging wildfire! Seek not their counsel nor their blessing!"

Anlaf glanced around the room, looking each man and woman in the eye, if they would lift their gaze to meet his. Some did. Some looked away, muttering. But no one argued. Not openly, at least. He suspected some of the muttering was defiance of his words, but he had to choose his battles. And he had won this battle. For now. Brow still creased with anger, he stalked from the building into the village square, sword in hand. Hugaldur the *godhi* stepped out into the cool air of winter's end a moment later. The two men stared at each other for a moment.

"You have my thanks, Anlaf," said Hugaldur after a moment, "That could have become a lot uglier pretty quickly, had you not intervened." Sweat stood out on Hugaldur's forehead despite the chill in the air.

"Aye," agreed Anlaf, exhaling a long breath he had not realized that he had been holding. He sheathed his sword. "For a moment there, I thought that I was going to have to *use* that." He chuckled ruefully at the thought.

"Have you ever had to use your sword before?" asked Hugaldur, who seemed genuinely curious.

"Never in the performance of my duties as alderman of Rorvik, nay. In my youth, I marched to war for the Skjoldungur king, and I did my share of killing in battle, of course. But I have never had to turn my sword on my neighbors before." Anlaf sighed. "I am glad I did not have to actually do that today, either. But for a moment, I really thought I might have to do it."

"What are you going to do now?" asked the priest, who was mopping the sweat from his brow with his sleeve.

"I plan to go home and eat. Then I am going to go investigate along the edge of the forest, near the standing stones. I feel sure that the killer, whoever or whatever that may be, has been working near the stones. Care to help, Hugi?"

The priest shook his head. "Good Freyur, no! No adventures for me, thank you! I'll pray for you, though!"

The alderman grimaced, and said, "Well, thanks for that, at least! If *you* cannot aid me, good Freyur surely must!"

"Do you blaspheme, good alderman?" asked Hugaldur in surprise.

"Of course not," sighed Anlaf bitterly, "I thank you again for your prayers. Be well, good Hugi!" With that, the alderman turned and stalked away towards his own homestead.

Not far from his dwelling, however, Anlaf was overwhelmed by the feeling that something was amiss. There was a salty, foul smell on the wind that he did not recognize at first, but which somewhat resembled the scents of the reedy seaside marshes on the edge of Rorvik. Then he realized that it was much like the odor he had smelt when he found Mother Sigurlaug's corpse. Hastening toward his home, Anlaf once more drew his sword, praying to Thorr that he would not need to use it, but not truly expecting to be so fortunate once again. As he came around the low stone structure roofed with thatching and sod, he saw that the door stood open, and a small volume of slimy marsh water had pooled on the threshold. He had sent Oddlaf home to keep her safe, but now . . .

Moving cautiously, Anlaf approached the door to his house. He almost called out, then paused and reconsidered. Ever since his wife had died a few winters earlier of a terrible fever that neither Mother Sigurlaug's herbs nor the prayer of the *godhar* seemed to touch, Anlaf had dwelt alone, but for his daughter. And Oddlaf spent so much time out with Arndis or working in the longhouse that he did not really see her much these days, either. There would be no one home except Oddlaf, unless some *intruder* had come . . .!

Sword at the ready, Anlaf stepped stealthily into the doorway of his home, feet planted apart to avoid the noisome pool of foul liquid at the threshold. His weary eyes scanned the dark interior of the small house, ears straining for the slightest sound. He had braced himself for an attack from the shadows that never came. There was nothing. No one home.

A chill passed through Anlaf's guts. *Where was his daughter? Where was Oddlaf?*

Coldly, Anlaf inspected the door and doorframe. The door had been left open. There was no visible damage to the area. No forced entry. It was as if Oddlaf had simply walked out the door and forgotten to close it. Except for the stench. Except for the pool of slimy water. Things were *not* right here, no matter how much Anlaf might wish he could dismiss it. Oddlaf had not simply forgotten to close the door, even had she been inclined to disobey his command to come home and bar the door. The evidence, such as it was, suggested she had been *taken*.

A cold fury now began to burn within Anlaf as he pondered this. *Taken.* Taken *where?*

All thought of waiting until the king's men came now fled. His *daughter* had been *taken.* Anlaf knew he was surely too old for this situation, and was not certain how he would have handled it even in his prime, but he knew he could not rest until he knew what had happened to Oddlaf and she was either safe or avenged. He looked down at the hand that held his sword and saw that his grip had turned his knuckles white. What had begun as a cold fury in his breast now began to burn white-hot.

How *dare* someone lay hand upon his daughter? Anlaf had never been gifted by Odhinn with the *berserkergang*, the red rage that made a man almost a divine instrument of uncontrolled fury in battle, but he felt it must be something similar to what he was experiencing now. He felt tremors of rage shudder through his limbs. *Where had they taken her?*

And then, stomach churning, Anlaf felt a sick certainty settle over his mind that he knew the answer. The glade of the standing stones, just outside the village - that had to be it. Any day now the morning sunlight would strike the Spring Stone at the correct angle, and it would be officially springtime. The villagers who had spoken of propitiating the Jotnar in order to appease their wrath - had one of them not said something about "blood of the sacrifice" needing to be on the Spring Stone before the equinox dawned? That *must* be it! The cultists of the Jotnar were going to sacrifice Oddlaf!

Anlaf spun around and began sprinting through the village towards the little path by the bay that led towards the glade of the standing stones. He gave brief thought to seeking help from the other villagers, but he quickly dismissed such notions from his mind. He didn't know for certain whom he could trust among the villagers, except for Hugaldur (who had already refused to aid him). He was on his own, "trusting in his own might and main," as the sagas would sing of a great hero. But Anlaf was no hero. He was just an old man who wanted his daughter back.

Anlaf tried to ignore the aches in his bones and pains in his joints as he turned onto the path that led toward the glade of the standing stones. Tightness gripped his chest, squeezing air from his lungs, causing his breath to come in ragged, jarring spurts. He knew he was *too old*, and he also knew he could not, *must not* stop, not now! Anlaf's boots pounded along the muddy path, sliding a little with each stride, so that he had to fight to keep balance. It kept him off-rhythm, unsure, unready. But this had to be done.

As he approached the hidden glade, Anlaf slowed his run to a jog and brought his sword up in a defensive stance. The fetid, swampy *smell* was back, renewing its reeking assault upon his nostrils - a stronger stench than before, if that were possible. The forest's shadows seemed deeper, darker than they ought to have been. The air seemed to almost *crackle* with an unseen yet palpable force. Surely there was dark sorcery at work in this place! Horror made the hair on the nape of Anlaf's neck stand up, and he wished he could close his eyes, but it was too late, now. He had arrived at the shadow-drenched glade.

Though the sun had been high in the sky when Anlaf entered the forest, darkness reigned here, doubtless given strength by some dark miracle or witchery. Through the gloom, Anlaf could see three black-robed figures, faces shrouded by heavy cowls, conducting some sort of ritual. Each had in hand an iron dagger stained with what was surely blood. Anlaf was about to bellow forth some sort of challenge, but even as he drew breath to shout, the robed figures shrieked some word of summoning. The summons was answered instantly: a huge, hulking humanoid figure stepped out of the darkened woods into the forest perpendicular to the path Anlaf trod.

The gruesome hulk seemed to be the source of the noxious stench. It dripped silty slime and fouled water from a flesh that seemed composed of mud, muck, and rotting vegetation. The being walked on two legs like a human, but there was something inhuman, something alien, about its every motion. Darkness seemed to pool in the air around it, just as fetid water pooled at its feet in the grass. Anlaf had no name for such a creature, but composed of raw elements as it was, he knew it was surely a creature of the Jotnar, the Lords of Ice and Fire. Whatever the thing was, it did not seem to notice Anlaf, nor did the robed figures who turned to great the swamp-beast's arrival.

The murky creature croaked and moaned in a voice like gravel grinding in a heavy surf, growling, "I have failed, masters, I was unable to seize the one for whom I was sent!"

"*What?* How dare you return without the sacrifice we demanded!" cried one of the robed figures in a harsh, feminine voice - one that was familiar, somehow, but it took a moment for Anlaf to place it out of context. Then he had it - it was Kolbrun, the fishwife, from the village. She pointed her blood-stained dagger in the direction of the swamp creature, as if threatening it somehow, and screeched, "Resume your hunt and do not return without your quarry! The blood of our sacrifice must be upon the stone before dawn tomorrow!"

Anlaf could bear no more, crying, "Kolbrun! What is this? Where is my daughter?"

The three robed folk turned towards Anlaf now, lowering their heavy cowls so they could see him better. Kolbrun was the leader, clearly, and she was flanked by a fisherman named Hofdhi and an elderly farmer named Kolur. Vefastur was not present, to Anlaf's considerable surprise given his role in the altercation back at the village longhouse, but that did not mean he was not part of the cult as well. All three cultists glared at Anlaf, lips curling back in feral snarls at his interruption. They hefted their bloody daggers, preparing to strike if he came near.

"I say *again*, Kolbrun - WHERE IS MY DAUGHTER?" roared Anlaf, shifting into a sword-fighting stance.

"Kill the interloper!" sneered Kolbrun. The swamp-monster shambled forward in obedience to Kolbrun's command, growling fiercely, while Hofdhi and Kolur scuttled backwards through the glade so as not to come between the creature and its prey. Anlaf found himself trembling with both fury and fear as the reeking thing advanced towards him. "We don't have your daughter - *yet!* But we shall soon find her!" taunted the old fishwife, "And then it will be *her* blood on the stones that saves Rorvik from a lingering winter!"

"But if *you* did not take her, where -?" Anlaf was unable to complete the question as the swamp monster lunged abruptly towards him, forcing him to slash furiously at the creature with his longsword. The creature's body was tough, but not indestructible; it felt much like blazing a trail through an overgrown bit of marsh, hacking through dense, wet plants and muck. The creature snarled, but otherwise did not slow down, forcing Anlaf to back away rapidly. His sword felt heavy in his hand, and he could not seem to catch his breath. Stumbling, exhausted, Anlaf forced himself to remain standing, believing that if he fell, it would mean Oddlaf's life as well as his own.

Suddenly, a vicious cry rang out through the glade from *behind* the cultists. Anlaf recognized his daughter's voice, and gave a wordless exclamation of astonishment, though he dared not divide his attention to look in her direction. The creature he battled occupied all of his attention - or, at least, it *had*. But now the beast stood still, frozen in place, allowing Anlaf to hack at it without defending itself. It looked *confused*, if such a word could apply to a lumpen mass of swamp-muck.

Meanwhile, Oddlaf had burst into the clearing from the opposite side, bearing a set of spears and shield. "I give your lives to Odhinn!" she cried out, casting a spear over the heads of the three robed cultists. Anlaf and the cultists shuddered, for this was a terrible rite of the ancient days - by calling upon Odhinn and throwing a spear over them, Oddlaf had asked for Odhinn's aid, and sworn to dedicate her foes as a sacrifice. She had just vowed not to profit by this battle in any way; everything they bore, no matter how precious, was part of her sacrifice to the god. Odhinn could claim the cultists' souls as *einherjar* for Valholl, whatever their former allegiance, if only he would grant Oddlaf aid in slaying them. As Kolur and Hofdhi turned to face her, Oddlaf rushed forward and rammer her spear through Kolur's guts, all three of them screaming.

Kolbrun had glanced at Oddlaf, but had dismissed her as something with which Kolur and Hofdhi could deal. She turned back to her champion, but found it still motionless, allowing Anlaf to hack away at it more boldly. "Why do you hesitate?" she screeched, "I ordered you to *kill him!*"

"True," the creature grated in its terrible voice, "But-, but-, but you *also* ordered me to find the girl and seize her! She is *right there!* He is *right here!* I-, I-, I *cannot* follow both your commands at once!" It took a jerking, shuddering step back, lifting an arm half-heartedly to ward off Anlaf's blade. Anlaf, putting what strength he had left into the stroke, swung the sword over his head and brought it down with a cry, lopping off the monster's outstretched arm.

"HELP ME!" wailed the monster piteously.

At the same moment, Oddlaf put her boot to the dying Kolur's chest and kicked him off the tip of her spear as his body began to slump to the ground. The flopping corpse tumbled backwards, causing Hofdhi to stumble as he rushed at the girl, dagger raised to strike. She whirled, bringing up the shield she bore.. The iron dagger clattered harmlessly against the scarred wooden surface, causing Hofdhi to curse loudly, and he tried to regain his balance for another stroke. But crouched behind the shield, Oddlaf now twisted her lithe body, bringing the spear to bear. She shoved the spear with all her might at Hofdhi's face, and was rewarded when the iron point slid into his left eye and up into his brain. The fisherman cultist twitched, his iron dagger dropping from suddenly nerveless fingers, and a new stench filled the air as he voided his bowels and collapsed.

"DEFEND YOURSELF!" screamed Kolbrun at her servitor, "Slay the alderman first; I'll deal with his brat until you are done!" A sick smile of triumph twisted her face as the creature began to move again, smashing its remaining fist into Anlaf, who had grown overconfident while the creature could not fight back.

Anlaf fell back hard. The punch had knocked the wind out of him, and he could not catch his breath. He had been finding it difficult to breathe *before* the massive blow to his chest. Pain wracked every nerve in his body, yet still he struggled to stand, to lift the sword again. He gritted his teeth and called out, "Fear not,

Oddlaf! I am coming to save you!" But an icy fear tore at his guts that he would soon be overwhelmed; he was truly too old for a fight like this.

"Nay, father, *I* am coming to save *you!*" yelled Oddlaf. Her spearpoint was lodged in Hofdhi's skull, and she found she could not easily yank it out, so she released her grip on the shaft. Kolbrun's wicked smile widened to see Oddlaf disarmed, but Oddlaf brought up her shield and rushed past Kolbrun, smashing the old fishwife to one side as she ran to her father's side.

The swamp creature had limped forward to stand over Anlaf in triumph. Anlaf twitched and flopped on the ground, trying desperately to stand, to fight, but gasping for breath and unable to push through the agony afflicting his every limb. The sword fell from Anlaf's grasp, and his hand flapped weakly at the hilt, unable to take it up again. The monster raised its one good arm of ropey vines and swamp-muck over its head, preparing to bring down its fist and smash Anlaf's skull.

But then, Oddlaf suddenly filled the creature's field of view, diving down between the beast and her father. She brought the shield up to defend Anlaf, and when the terrible fist came down, it struck only wood. But the shield cracked and splintered from the blow, and Oddlaf shrieked in pain as the impact broke the arm that bore the shield as well. With an inhuman chuckle, the beast stepped forward and prepared to strike again. Anlaf sobbed, cowering, unable to open his eyes.

Oddlaf felt the fingers of her right hand curl around the hilt of Anlaf's sword, a rage like she had never known kindling her soul. "Do not fear, father!" she whispered, then leapt up, releasing the shield from her broken arm and swinging her father's blade in a horizontal arc that sliced cleanly through the monster's misshapen head. She realized that the scream that filled her ears was her own as the beast let out a gargling, crying wail from somewhere deep within its torso. The thing collapsed into a stinking pile of rotting muck as whatever life had been conjured into it by the cultists fled forever.

"That is *impossible!*" screamed Kolbrun, trembling in terror as she watched her creature dissolve.

"Odhinn take you," said Oddlaf coldly as she swung her father's blade one more time. Kolbrun's head rolled across the grassy floor of the glade as the fishwife's head tumbled heavily to the ground. It was over.

Anlaf vomited, shaking, then uncurled his body and tried to catch his breath again. It came in great, sobbing shudders, but it came. He wiped his mouth on his sleeve and opened his eyes, looking at Oddlaf standing over Kolbrun's corpse. "I'm so *happy* to see you, daughter," he wept, "I thought they might have already slain you, and that all that remained was to avenge you!" His struggled to rise to his feet. He was so *weak*.

"I'm so sorry, father," said Oddlaf, "I *did* try to obey you! I went home, just like you said. But before I got there, I stopped at Arndis' house. I knew you had sent her on to Hleidhra, but I thought I could borrow a shield and some spare spears in case we had any more trouble. Erna said it would be all right if I borrowed Arndis' gear! But by the time I got home . . . well, I saw that *thing* shambling towards our house, so I hid and watched it break in. I thought it was looking for *you!* When it did not find us at home, it lumbered away toward the glade, here. I figured that this must be where it was heading, so I circled around through the woods so I could come up on whomever was here by surprise!"

"Well, you certainly surprised *me*, dearest daughter," croaked Anlaf, "I thought I had to save you, but-"

"But I had already saved myself. And then you," smiled Oddlaf, "And now . . ."

"Aye, now," grunted Anlaf, "Now we'll have to build a pyre for these corpses and all their gear. You dedicated them to Odhinn, so you know you have to sacrifice it all, aye?" He saw her nod gravely. "Good," he continued, "We'll have to announce what happened, and send *another* rider to Hleidhdra. With luck, there are no more secret worshipers of the Lords of Ice and Fire hiding in our village! And then . . ."

"Then, one more thing," said Oddlaf. "I want you to teach me to use *this*," she said hefting his sword in her hand. "I was lucky, these cravens knew as little of fighting as I. And I had Odhinn watching over me, for my promise of sacrifice. But if I had needed to face a trained warrior? We would both be dead."

Anlaf groaned, taking a shaky step towards his daughter and putting his arm around her. Earlier that day, he had been reflecting upon how glad he was that his daughter had no taste for fighting and adventure, that he could keep her safe. And that he had never needed to draw his sword against his neighbors before. But now . . .

"Agreed," he grunted, seeing his daughter smile. "You should learn. You seem to have some natural talent, and that is good, but you should still learn. You'll have to wait until your shield-arm heals, and that may take some time, now that Mother Sigurlaug is gone. Maybe Hugaldur can say some prayers of healing for you. But once your arm is whole again, I'll teach you what I know."

"Thank you, father," said Oddlaf. "Now help me gather wood for a pyre, please," she said, "My broken arm will not make it easy to do what is needful, and it turns out that we have a sacrifice to make, after all."

9. FAR FROM THE TREE

Hrafn the Runecaster paused his endless trudging through the forest thickly blanketing the foothills of the Jarnhryggur Mountains of western Svialand, and he knelt down on the ground among the decaying leaves and pine needles. The dark blue rune-embroidered cloak that kept the worst of the wind from his body settled around his crouching form like the wings of the raven for which he was named, in the Thjodhiskmal tongue of the North. With one hand he cleared a space on the ground, with the other he took a small, soft leather pouch from his belt and placed it before him. Every sense he had, both natural and mystical, told him that he was going the right way. But he had to be *sure.*

Muttering prayers for guidance, Hrafn reached into his leather pouch and drew from it a handful of wooden tiles inscribed with runes. One by one, he placed the tiles on the cleared ground and took careful note. *Aye. This is the way.* He scooped up the wooden tokens and placed them back into his little sack, then returned that sack to his belt.

He was close to his destination. He could feel it, almost *taste* it in the air. The Hidden Orchard.

Leaning heavily on his ashwood runestaff, Hrafn pulled himself upright again, joints creaking. *How did I get so old?* He gazed off into the forest, but he could see nothing but trees and bushes, swaying gently in the chill wind. *It does not matter whether or not I can see it. It is near. That is all I need to know.*

With a deep sigh, Hrafn began to walk again. This kind of rough travel through the autumn wilderness had been easier decades ago. He knew he ought to be used to it by now, but the problem wasn't that he was unaccustomed to the rigors of surviving the wilds of the North, or even the harshness of the season (and, in truth, it had been a mild autumn, for the North). The problem was that his body was beginning to fail him, slowly, as age ate away at his vigor and vitality. His will grew ever stronger, but his flesh and bone weakened.

Still he walked on, boots whispering through the fallen leaves and needles, for Hrafn believed - no, he *knew* - that the will is more powerful than mere matter. His powers as a magician proved that; his will could change reality itself, with the right runes and spells. So he would not allow being *tired* to slow him down.

A cliff wall loomed ahead, bursting with jagged stones and crevices, but Hrafn could see a path that looked like it would take him to the top. Without hesitation, he began to climb the narrow path. *If I fear the path, and let it stop me, then I am done. I must not stop.* The path was even more arduous than it had appeared at first, and still Hrafn labored onwards, up the cliff. He knew he was almost there.

And then, suddenly, somehow, he had reached the top, and the narrow way broadened into a gentle, flat path of stone. Trees and boulders loomed to either side, but it was as if a tunnel had been dug straight through this part of the forest. Ahead, walls of stone closed in, as if forming a narrow gateway into the mountains. Hrafn took a moment to suck in great lungfuls of cool, thin mountain air, grateful to be walking level ground instead of climbing. His rune-carved staff clattered along the stone surface as he walked, but it helped him keep his balance. *Is this it?*

All at once, Hrafn's nostrils caught a delicious scent wafting on the breezes blowing from the stone gateway ahead - *apples!* The Hidden Orchard was *here*! Hrafn redoubled his pace as he strode forward, knowing the end of his long, lonely trek was in sight. *Almost there, at last!*

When the figure of a gray-robed man armed with a runestaff stepped into the breach in the cliffs ahead of him, Hrafn was not actually surprised. He had, in fact, been expecting the guardian of this place to show himself some time ago. The surprise, he thought to himself, was that the guardian of the Hidden Orchard should take so long to reveal himself. Hrafn saw that the man was beardless, as he himself was, an oddity in the North where men tended to pride themselves on their beards. He halted his progress and stood calmly, waiting.

The beardless, gray-robed guardian wore a tall, wide-brimmed hat, and his ashwood staff was as wound about with carved runes and spells as Hrafn's own. He took a confident step toward Hrafn, then hesitated, and took another, more cautious one. The man stood a short distance away, blocking passage to the Hidden Orchard with his body, studying Hrafn's face with piercing eyes that glared out from under the wide brim of his hat. Those pale blue eyes bore a remarkable similarity to Hrafn's own.

"Ah," the man said, "I see. You know who I am, then?"

"Aye," replied Hrafn, his voice as steady as he could make it, "You are Heruli, reputed to be the greatest runecaster in the history of Midhgardhur, are you not?"

The man nodded solemnly, then said, "And you . . . you are one of mine. I can see it in your face. Which one are you?" Heruli, for that was indeed his name, had the good grace to look slightly embarrassed to have to ask this question.

Hrafn straightened himself and stared back defiantly, his pale blue gaze meeting Heruli's, and said, "My mother was named Ulfhildur; she lived and died not far from Uppsalir. She named me Hrafn. Hrafn Herulason. Finnur of Uppsalir was my master in the mysteries of the runes. And I believe I am your son."

Heruli nodded sadly. "I remember your mother. She knew that she was with child before I left her farm, but I never . . . She said that she understood that I had to move on. I hope that she did not hate me."

"She always spoke well of you, father," replied Hrafn, "She *did* understand. But she always hoped you might return someday. As did I." He choked on these last words.

Heruli tightened his grip on his staff, and said, "And you, son? Did *you* hate me? Do you?"

Hrafn sighed. "For a time, I suppose that I did," he replied, "As a child, I was bitter for our poverty, and for the lack of a father in my life. But I grew wise and clever, and found it easy to learn strange and cunning things, and my mother said that those things were legacies from your blood. So when I came of age, I went to Uppsalir and offered myself as apprentice to Finnur the Runecaster . . . he would have refused me, for my mean resources . . . but then I told him you were my father, and he took me on. Your name opened doors to me that might otherwise have stood closed forever. Even absent, you gave me much. Nay, I do not hate you. Not now."

Heruli nodded slowly, but did not relax his guard. "Why have you sought me out, then, son? Or is it the Orchard that you seek?" His appraising gaze ran up and down Hrafn's blue-cloaked body. They might have seemed to be of an age - or, if anything, Heruli might have been Hrafn's junior by a decade or more. He had a strange, ageless quality to his features, and an unsettlingly spry way of moving his body for a man as old as he had to be.

Hrafn licked his lips and paused before he answered. "It is true, then? It is here?"

"The Hidden Orchard? Oh, aye. It is here. But you did not answer the question I asked. Or was that the answer, in truth?" said Heruli.

"Both," replied Hrafn, "Truly, I sought *you* first, but then I began to come across legends that said the Hidden Orchard was where I might find you, and so I sought the Orchard. After years of research and exploration, I began to think it was right here in Svialand, in the wild places, where few would think to look. After so many years, when I had my first real clues to the Hidden Orchard's location . . . well, let us say that by then, I hoped to find the place as much as I had longed to complete my original quest."

"Well, you are here, at last," said Heruli slowly, "So I suppose you had better come with me." He turned and walked through the natural rock gate. Hrafn could now see that the opening led to a small, hidden valley full of trees. "Come along!" called Heruli's voice.

With slow, cautious steps, Hrafn approached the gap that led to the hidden valley. His instincts were to trust nothing and no one, so all his senses scanned everything about him, prepared to fight his way out of a potential trap. But it seemed there was no trap. Just the scent of apples wafting from a secret valley in the mountains. Half unthinking, he tapped with his staff like a blind man, testing the ground before him as he slowly entered the valley.

It was real. The Hidden Orchard. Apple trees filled the small, enclosed valley, apple trees laden with shining crimson and golden fruit, past ready for harvest. It was real, and it was *here*. The land had been tended by the hand of man, that much was plain - Hrafn supposed that was part of his father's role in this place, after all - yet it somehow felt *primal* and *wild* here, as if it were a site not meant for the tread of human feet.

Seeing his son standing dumbfounded, with his mouth gaping open, Heruli quietly asked, "You know the story, then? How this place came to be?" He saw his son nod, slowly. "Tell me then," he said, "what is the story that you heard?"

Hrafn turned to look at his father, startled back to his senses by the question. "Now?" he asked.

"Now," agreed Heruli.

Hrafn cleared his throat, then began: "Long ago, in the early ages of the Nine Worlds, they say that the Jotunn named Thjazi had captured the god Loki and arranged with him to steal the apples of the goddess Idhunn - the apples of youth and immortality, the food of the gods. Loki lured Idhunn out of Asgardhur and brought her to a secret place in the forest here on Midhgardhur where he claimed that he had found apples like hers. He convinced her to bring her apples to compare them to what he had found. That hidden spot is supposed to be right here, where we are standing.

"When they arrived here, Idhunn discovered that there were no apple trees, and she angrily demanded to know what was going on. She prepared to storm away back to Asgardhur, but suddenly, Thjazi swooped out of the sky in the form of a giant eagle, and snatched her away with her magic apples.

"The rest of the story is not really important - essentially, the gods began to age and notice that Idhunn was missing, and they remembered that she was last seen leaving Asgardhur with Loki, so they arrested him. They managed to get out of him what he had done, and threatened him with dire punishments for his crime, but he convinced them to give him a chance to make it right. Eventually, he succeeded in bringing Idhunn and her apples back to Asgardhur, and they even manage to slay Thjazi in the bargain. But there is a curious legend about the brief time that Loki and Idhunn were here.

"It is said that when Thjazi swooped down and seized Idhunn and her apples, a couple of the magical apples fell to the ground here, in this valley. The enchanted seeds eventually took root in the more mundane soil of Midhgardhur, and produced an orchard of apple trees far from the tree in Asgardhur that bore the apples. The Hidden Orchard. Because *these* apples are not growing in the divine soil of Asgardhur, but soak up mere mortality from the dirt of our world, they have nowhere near as much power as the ones possessed by the goddess Idhunn. But because the seeds were of divine origin, they do retain a degree of enchantment. They can grant youth to the aging, and longer life, to a point; not true immortality, as the Apples of Idhunn are said to give, but a greater measure of vitality, to be sure. That is why I look younger than you do, my son."

Hrafn nodded. "But how did you come to be the guardian of this place, father? Are you all alone here?"

Heruli's eyes glistened, as if he were holding back tears of sorrow, as he replied, "Alone? Aye, I am alone, now. I have fared far and wide across Midhgardhur, my son, and I have had great friends and companions on my journeys. But they all leave in the end, one way or another. The last of my companions was a *lytlingur,* a halfling named Tholmann from Jorvikskyr. He traveled with me for decades, he brought me good fortune and companionship, but in the end he settled down and bought an inn. He was always more at home in a kitchen than in the wilderness or in the depths of ancient dungeons, anyway. It was just a few years ago that he went back to Jorvikskyr and I returned to this place. That is how my journeys always seem to end.

"But you also asked how I came to guard the Hidden Orchard! It happened longer ago than you might think! I was not born with the name I now bear; it was once the name of my tribe, a people long vanished from the face of Midhgardhur. I was not born here in Svialand, but to the south, long ago, when the Heruli were among the Gauthioth tribes in the time of their great struggle with the Norrani Imperium. My people went to war with that demon-plagued empire, and we rode south to besiege them in their own lands.

"The Norrani were so civilized, but they were also corrupt and decadent. We free folk of the Gauthioth had once held the knowledge and wisdom of their ancient civilization in wonder, but with the passing of centuries we learned to hold their cruelty and wickedness in contempt. And so our wars with them had seemed inevitable to us, at the time. I was a very young man when the shamans of the Heruli sensed in me the spark, the inborn power, to learn the great mysteries. The Norrani invoked terrible sorceries in their wars against our people, and in return our most gifted people brought the mysteries of our own to bear against them.

"I may not speak of my initiation to power in detail. I had mine, as you have no doubt had your own, Hrafn! But I can say that when

I was initiated, I had a vision of the runes, just as Odhinn did when he hanged himself from Yggdrasill to gain that sacred knowledge, which has been passed down to poor mortals such as us! But along with the vision that burned the runes into my mind and soul, I also had a vision of the Hidden Orchard, and how to find it. I knew that I had to seek it out someday.

"At length, the tribe of the Heruli were successful in our campaigns against the crumbling Norrani Imperium. Their outer provinces fell, one by one, and then some of us joined an army of Gauthioths marching on the city of Norra herself. But I felt the call to seek out the Orchard in my vision, and so I turned North as most of the tribe went south. I never heard from them again. I went on my way alone.

"When I first came to the Hidden Orchard, the trees were withered, beginning to die. They had been left untended for long ages of the world, probably since the times when Loki still walked free upon Midhgardhur, before the death of Baldur. The Orchard was overgrown with vines and other plants, and they were finally beginning to choke out the apple trees. But I worked for months to bring the Orchard back to full life, and the apples from the trees restored my full life to me.

"Since that time, I have not always remained here. Far from it! I have often ventured forth on business of my own throughout Midhgardhur over the centuries. I have battled demons and dragons, helped topple and raise kingdoms, loved and lost, over and over. I earned my reputation as one of the greatest, if not the greatest, runecaster in all of Midhgardhur. But in the end, I always return to the Hidden Orchard, and here I rest and labor until I am restored and ready to venture forth again."

Hrafn looked solemn. Then, slowly, he turned around, gazing at all the magnificent splendor of this hidden grove. "Aye," he said at last, "But what happens when you leave the Orchard? Who tends the trees when you are gone?"

"There has never been another I could trust with the secret," replied Heruli, "so I trust to luck and the favor of the gods for the preservation of the Orchard in my absence. Mayhaps sometime I shall return to find the Orchard in ruin, and I shall finally grow old and die."

"Mayhaps you shall, at that," said Hrafn thoughtfully, "I think that is as it is meant to be. I wish to eat of the apples here, father, and regain something of my youth and vitality. Is that permitted?"

Heruli gave Hrafn a grim smile that Hrafn was uncomfortably aware was very much like his own. "I am under no obligation to stop others from partaking of the sacred fruit of the Orchard, son. You may eat of this fruit; it is permitted. But consider well what you will do with the gift of youth restored! To have your vitality restored without purpose can be a very dangerous thing. It can drive men mad."

Reverently, Hrafn reached out and plucked a shining apple from a tree. Lifting it to his mouth, he took a large bite with a *crunch* that echoed through the silent Orchard. The heavenly scent filled his nostrils, and the sweet, divine flavor filled his mouth. He smiled, feeling his body flood with a warmth that washed away the aching in his joints and muscles, the creaking in his bones. Then Hrafn turned to his father. "I have tasks enough to keep me busy for lifetimes," he said, "and I do not fear the prospect of having time and strength to pursue them all.

"I suppose that you might expect that I would offer to exchange places with you. That one of us could stay and guard the Hidden Orchard while the other is off questing around Midhgardhur. But this I shall not do. I shall help tend the Hidden Orchard while I am here, for that is only right. But I shall leave in my own good time, as you have done and will do again. And if no one is here to guard the Orchard, then so be it. And if ill should befall the Orchard, so be it. Whatever strength we may gain from this place is a gift, but a gift that is given us, and may be withdrawn at any time by *wyrd,* by fate. It is not for us to ensure that we shall always be given whatever we desire."

Heruli smiled. "That is the risk that I have taken every time I have left this place for centuries now. And it seems right that we continue to take that risk together. If one wishes to change the world, one must risk losing everything. Aye, you are much like me, after all. It is as they say. The apples does not fall far from the tree."

10. THE GORGONADES SHIPWRECK

Radhvaldur swallowed seawater and prayed to Ran, goddess of drowned men, that she not drag him down to her realm. *Let this not be my end!*

A storm raged all around, black clouds stretched to the horizons in all directions, as deafening thunder boomed directly overhead. The storm had come from nowhere, or so it had seemed, but no Northerner had ever sailed these waters and returned to boast of it, so who could say what was normal or natural under these strange skies? As far as the crew of the Uxinn knew, they were the first Northerners to sail out of the sheltered sea of the South they called the Midhjardharhaf, through the straits called the Pillars of Melkartes, and into the southern reaches of the Promethean Ocean, turning south along the coast of the mysterious continent of Omuria.

The wave that had swept Radhvaldur from the deck of the Uxinn, had looked like an enormous green-black wall rushing towards them at impossible speed. Like falling from a great height toward a dark, rich land, only *sideways*. And when the water struck, it was just like hitting the ground after falling from a great height . . .

Radhvaldur could not even see the ship anymore. He knew he had been lucky he had not been wearing his armor when the storm hit, or he would already serve in Ran's halls. Even the sword buckled at his waist threatened to drag him down, but was willing to struggle against its added weight for now. *Where was the ship?* Was the Uxinn still afloat, somehow, or had it been sunk, perhaps shattered by a thunderbolt from above, or smashed against hidden rocks in these unfamiliar waters? *In the name of Njordhur, where was the bloody ship?*

A belly full of seawater – he simply could not avoid swallowing some whenever he tried to breathe! - and a swelling sense of panic that he was going to drown in this unfamiliar, uncanny Southern ocean made Radhvaldur feel about as ill as he had ever felt in his life. Being tossed about like a child's doll by monstrous waves was not helping either. He could not breathe, he could barely stay above water, he could not see the ship from which he had fallen, and he was retching up more seawater and panicked bile, filling his mouth with foulness. He would not last long on the open ocean in a storm without finding the Uxinn, if it somehow survived.

Titanic winds swept the waves, and in his despair Radhvaldur realized that the Uxinn could easily have been blown *miles* from him by now. Even if the ship survived, it was likely that it could not save him now.

Radhvaldur knew that he had to swim for shore if he were to live. But he could see no shore. He could not even guess in what direction the coast might lie. There was no hope, he knew it in his bones. Even if he unbuckled his sword belt, and let it slip down into the lightless depths below him, he would not have the strength to swim to land. Even Njordhur, Vanic god of sea and sailors, would not save him now. He was surely damned, doomed to Ran's realm of the drowned!

Despite his despair, Radhvaldur was born to a people not given to easy surrender, no matter how hopeless the situation. Gritting his teeth, lungs pumping like bellows, Radhvaldur forced himself to swallow another retch, picked a direction, and began to swim, his mighty muscles pitched in direct combat with the elements of sea and storm. He began to move, he was sure, slowly, very slowly, but he was moving forward. He could only pray it was towards land.

An eternity of agony passed as Radhvaldur stretched his

strength and endurance to their limits. *How long can I continue like this? Yet if I cannot, what other choice do I have?* Suddenly, however, the Northerner thought he could see a light burning in the distance. Whether it was land or a light aboard a ship, Radhvaldur could not guess, but it gave him a goal, when he had thought hope had drowned forever. He adjusted his course and strained his exhausted muscles to propel himself towards the distant flicker.

"I may yet survive!" he thought triumphantly, but just as Radhvaldur completed the thought, the surging sea brought floating debris crashing all around him. He had just enough time to wonder whether any of the timbers he saw were from the Uxinn when a wave brought a huge piece of wooden debris crashing down on the back of his head, and blackness welled up like the water of the lowest depths to claim his mind.

***

Radhvaldur awoke to a world of pain. The back of his skull, where the timber struck him; all of his muscles in his arms and legs and back, from straining to swim against the storm. But those aches felt old, stale, like they had been sitting out for a while. As Radhvaldur's mind swam towards consciousness like a drowning man trying to reach the surface of the water, clawing desperately upwards towards the light, other sensations of his body began to filter through the murk of dreamless sleep.

Pain. Pain in his wrists, which were held above his head, where Radhvaldur slowly realized metal was digging into his skin. Manacles. He was chained like a thrall, in a dungeon. Hunger. He had not eaten in – how long now? How long had he been unconscious?

Radhvaldur opened his eyes. Not complete darkness, but very dim. He was chained to a stone wall. Though the stones were closely-fitted, moss grew in the mortaring, indicating the dungeon was an old one. He pulled, wincing as the metal manacles dug deeper into his flesh and clanked in the darkness. The chains were thick, but they were old and rusty. With time, he might be able to get loose.

He did not have time. Radhvaldur heard the squeal of hinges as a door opened somewhere, and heard the tramp of hobnailed boots coming towards him. Six men came around a corner, one of them bearing a torch which gave some illumination to the dungeon.

They were short, but this did not surprise Radhvaldur; most men in Midhgardhur were shorter than those of the North. They were muscular, with sun-bronzed skin, and their clothing and arms were strange, like those worn by statues he had seen in the Palnorran capital, the Silver City. All but one wore archaic iron breastplates and greaves, with vicious shortswords sheathed at their sides. The only one who was not so armed interested Radhvaldur the most.

The man wore the ancient draperies of Palnorran nobility, and his face bore the aristocratic features of that nation. But how did Palnorrans come to be *here?* They generally occupied the eastern end of their inland sea. What were they doing beyond the Pillars of Melkartes, which marked the *western* end of that sea, in the vast unknown Promeathean Ocean?

The strangers muttered softly among themselves, thinking Radhvaldur could not understand. But as he listened to them, he realized he *could*, based on the Palnorrani he had learned in the Silver City. Oh, it was different from what he had learned – more archaic, more complex, with a pronunciation that sounded slurred to his ears. But it was a language he knew. He cleared his throat and demanded, "Who are you? Where am I? Why are you holding me prisoner?"

The men gasped and stared in surprise. The apparent leader, the one without armor, recovered first, chuckling softly at the surprise on the faces of his men. "You speak our tongue! That makes things easier! My name is Demetrios, and you are trespassing on one of the islands of the Gorgonades, a land our ancestors won at great cost from the . . . *natives.* By our ancient tradition, all barbarians who trespass here must die."

The Gorgonades! He had seen some dubious charts produced in Gaunorria which blended what little the cartographers knew with ancient myth and artistic fancy. The Gorgonades were islands, out at the edge of the map. *What is it they write in Norrani at the margins of their maps? "HIC SUNT MONSTRA" - "here there be monsters" - well, why not? Who knew what monsters one might find off the edge of Midhgardhur, so far South that one must be nearing the world of Muspellsheimur, the World of Fire?*

"But I have done nothing wrong! What of the rites of *xenia*, of hospitality, to which I am entitled as a stranger to these shores?"

Demetrios looked grim as he answered, "You are entitled to nothing. The ancient god Dios Xenios, guarantor of hospitality, cursed this land and turned his face from it, so we turn our faces from him also. There is but one goddess on this island, and you will see her face soon enough. There is no protection for strangers, here."

"So you will kill me? Which of you would like to try that?" Radhvaldur twisted into the best fighting stance he could. A man could not escape his death if the Norns decreed it, but he could sell his life as dearly as possible. He had his feet, his teeth - even the iron chains that bound him could be weapons!

"A fierce one! *She* will be amused!" said Demetrios to his guards. They moved carefully around Radhvaldur and began to unbolt his chains from the wall. Demetrios smiled unpleasantly at Radhvaldur. "Let me tell you what is going to happen to you! In a moment, we are going to open the iron door a few feet to your left. It leads out of this fort. Then we are going to send one of the last surviving *natives* out there with you. Kill her, and you may live. Fail, and your life ends today."

The guards opened the gate and led him thence by his chains, they cast him through the portal to the sandy ground. A few feet away, he saw his sword planted in the earth – he had thought it lost in the shipwreck, consigned to the realm of Aegir and Ran forever! Then the iron door closed behind him.

Radhvaldur found himself standing in the shadow of a stone fortress, ringed by high walls of cyclopean stone covered in vines and moss. It must have been mid-morning, but the light was intolerably bright to Radhvaldur after his sojourn in the dungeon. The air was hot, humid, and very still. He blinked against the oppressive sunlight. Brightly colored, strongly-scented flowers of an unfamiliar sort bloomed from some of the vines. But what demanded Radhvaldur's attention were the statues.

Statues! Everywhere Radhvaldur looked, there were incredibly lifelike statues; all of them of unpainted, plain white marble, gleaming in the sun. They seemed to represent people of all sizes, nations, races, all of them carved with a preternatural attention to detail. Were they not so obviously composed of stone, Radhvaldur would have expected them to move and speak.

A moment later, Radhvaldur heard the chorused shout of the Palnorrans behind their iron portal: "RELEASE THE GORGON!"

The *gorgon!* The legendary creature for which these islands were named! Radhvaldur knew, now, his intended fate, and understood the origins of those too-perfect statues – they were not carved by sculptors, but were formed from once-living men and women! The grinding of another gate opening behind him confirmed that *something* had been released, and the hissing sound of myriad serpents suggested that it was as bad as Radhvaldur feared, but he dared not turn to look.

Radhvaldur took a deep breath. He knew that he was expected to look, and join the statues, or else refuse to look, so he would not be able to fight and thus be slain by the *gorgon.* The Northerners believed that when the Norns decreed death for any one, there was no escaping it – they would die whether they were brave or not when the time came, so it was better to be brave. He closed his eyes and faced the *gorgon* hunting him.

Eyes closed, Radhvaldur could not *see* the *gorgon.* But he could *hear* it – the terrible hissing of its serpentine hair, the growl in its almost-human throat, its footfalls as it ran at him. He fell to his knees on the sand and swung his blade, praying to Tyr, god of the sword, that it would strike true.

Radhvaldur knew his stroke had failed, meeting no resistance as it whirled though the space where he had believed the beast to be. Angry hissing told him that the *gorgon* had closed in, probably so that he could not use his sword well. Radhvaldur might hit it with a backswing, but he would not be able to put nearly as much strength into it.

In that moment, Radhvaldur knew what he had to do. If he was fated to die this day, then there was no altering that fact. Eyes clamped tightly shut against the possibility of a lethal glimpse, Radhvaldur raised his blade as if to threaten the *gorgon*. The *gorgon's* claws locked onto his arm, preventing him from bringing his sword to bear. When he felt that horrid grip on his right arm, he lashed out with his left, grappling the unseen creature's head, pulling it towards him. He felt the sting of its serpent hair biting into his flesh, over and over. Nevertheless, he pulled the *gorgon* to him, then lunged forward with his jaws, closing his teeth around the flesh of its throat. He bit as hard as he could, then bit again. And again.

Foul ichor sprayed him, but Radhvaldur ripped and tore, even as the serpentine hair stung his hand, arm, and face. He and the *gorgon* rolled onto the sand, locked together; he ripped at its throat like some savage wolf, as if he were some inhuman thing that fought with tooth and claw, not steel. The *gorgon's* thrashing became more frantic, then faded as its life drained away from its ruined veins and arteries. At last, the creature went limp, and Radhvaldur collapsed atop its corpse.

When Radhvaldur finally caught his breath, he felt that where the *gorgon's* hair had bit him, his flesh burned like fire. He could not look, for he guessed that even glimpsing a *dead gorgon* would kill him. He turned away from the corpse, opening his eyes at last.

Radhvaldur could see the ocean! He wanted nothing more than to bathe his wounds and battered limbs in the seawater. He had survived the Gorgonades shipwreck. Once he recovered, he would seek vengeance. And a way off the island.

ABOUT THE AUTHOR

Colin Brodd grew up in the great state of Rhode Island and Providence Plantations, but currently resides in Phoenix, Arizona. His business cards read "Gentleman Classicist Extraordinaire." He has held many different positions in his life, but his main professional calling has always been a teacher of Latin and Classical Humanities. In addition to Latin and Ancient Greek, he enjoys working with Old English and Old Norse and other old Germanic languages. His favorite genres of fiction are fantasy and science fiction, and he has a great love of RPGs (role-playing games). His favorite nonfiction books tend to be classical and military history or linguistics and languages (especially the aforementioned Greek and Latin). He sincerely appreciates your interest in his work.

AUTHOR'S NOTE

I cannot thank you enough for taking a chance and checking out my work! My self-published work depends on word-of-mouth to succeed, and I can really use your help! If you enjoyed my work, please let people know, especially on social media – blogs, Twitter, Facebook, and any other way you can! Reviews on Amazon and Goodreads would also be greatly appreciated! Please check out the following:

The award-winning Tales From Midhgardhur series is on Channillo - https://channillo.com/series/tales-from-midhgardhur/

Join the official fan club, Einherjar of Midhgardhur, on Facebook: https://www.facebook.com/groups/397155457403258/

Website: http://colinandersbrodd.wixsite.com/midhgardhur

Author Blog: http://colinandersbrodd.blogspot.com/

Facebook: www.facebook.com/ColinBroddBooks

Twitter: https://twitter.com/Midhgardhur

Tumblr: https://www.tumblr.com/blog/colin-anders-brodd

Instagram: https://www.instagram.com/midhgardhur.books/

Pinterest: https://www.pinterest.com/midhgardhur/

The Saga of Asa Oathkeeper:
https://www.amazon.com/dp/1533601348/

Tales From Midhgardhur, Volume I:
https://www.amazon.com/dp/1533614539/

Tales From Midhgardhur, Volume II:
https://www.amazon.com/dp/1979133344/

If you like me, you could also just buy me a coffee at:

ko-fi.com/midhgardhur

Thank you again for making my work possible! Happy reading! Skál!

~ Colin Anders Brodd

Made in the USA
San Bernardino, CA
08 March 2020